T5-DHJ-814

Mystery of the Scorpion Threat

The Dallas O'Neil Mysteries

MYSTERY OF THE SCORPION THREAT

by

JERRY B. JENKINS

MOODY PRESS

CHICAGO

© 1988 by
JERRY B. JENKINS

All rights reserved. No part of this book may be reproduced in any form without permission in writing from the publisher, except in the case of brief quotations embodied in critical articles or reviews.

ISBN: 0-8024-8379-8

1 2 3 4 5 6 Printing/LC/Year 92 91 90 89 88

Printed in the United States of America

To Gerry Stephenson

Contents

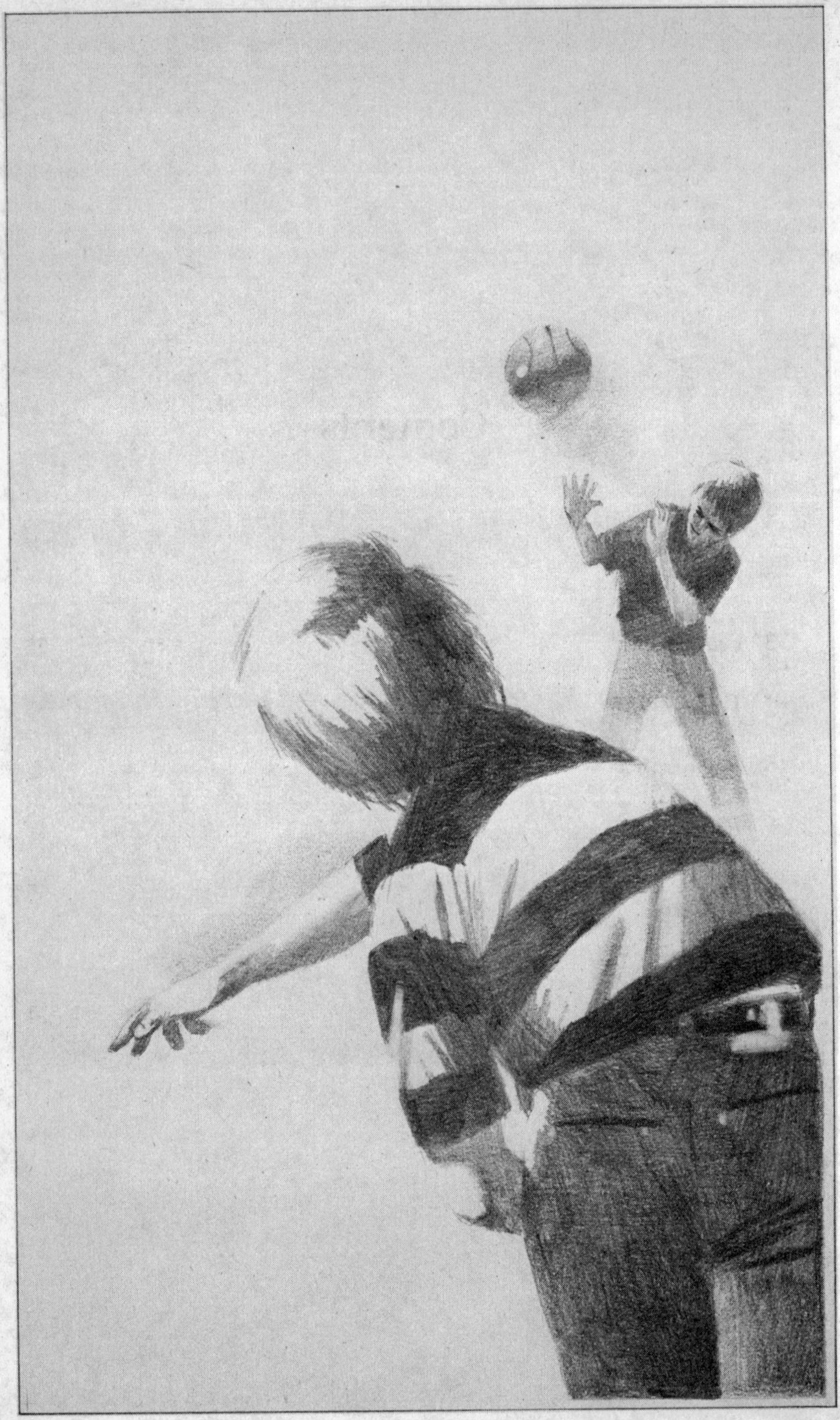

1

Ryan's Problem

It wasn't the first time I had to defend Ryan, and I knew it wouldn't be the last. He was the smallest kid in the Baker Street Sports Club, a blond who was considered cute by most of the girls at our school. He was in fifth grade, one grade behind me.

We were playing basketball out on the blacktop at recess, and Ryan was the only fifth grader in the game. Our sixth grade class was playing the other sixth grade class, and we were one player short. We asked the others if they minded if we used a fifth grader.

They said it was OK, and from the looks on their faces we could tell they thought we were out of our minds. It was hard enough to beat them with five sixth-graders, let alone four sixth-graders and a fifth-grader. And when we chose Ryan, they laughed.

Everyone knew that Jimmy and Cory and I played on the Baker Street Sports Club team and that we were all starters along with Bugsy and Jack, who went to different schools. What they didn't know was that Ryan had become our best sixth man. The year before he had ridden the bench most of the year, though we knew he was something special.

In practice he was a most unusual player, a ball-handling and shooting point guard who loved to follow up his shots on offense and wasn't afraid to fight for rebounds on defense. Though he was small, he could outjump Jimmy and Cory, and he had perfect timing and knew where to play as well as anyone on our team.

This year, whenever we brought him into a game (usually late in the first quarter), he replaced Jimmy at one of the forwards. I would switch from guard to forward with Cory, and Bugsy would switch from point guard to regular to relax a little. Jack was our center.

Instead of coasting with one of our starters out, we always picked up the pace a little. By that time, Bugsy and I were tired and needed the switch, and Ryan was ready to fly. He'd bring the ball up, set up the plays, do his share of shooting, and amaze everyone with more than his share of rebounding.

In a pickup game between the sixth graders, Jimmy and Cory and I were, of course, the most experienced players. The other player from our class was Nathaniel, a hulky kid who was a couple of years older than everyone else and should have been in eighth grade. He really didn't make much difference in the game. He was slow and a poor shooter, so the other class didn't care that we used him.

Our usual fifth man was the smartest kid in the class. He wasn't much of a basketball player, but he understood the game and was as good as anyone on the other team. But this day he was out sick, so we got permission to use Ryan. I was thrilled. They'd probably never let us use him again, once they saw what he could do, but meanwhile this was going to be fun.

I gathered the other four around me and asked them if they really wanted to enjoy this.

"Sure!"

"Then let's put Nat at center, Cory and Jimmy at the forwards, and Ryan and I will be the guards. For the first few minutes, I'll be point guard, and Ryan will just coast. When we need some fire power, Ryan and I will switch. They won't know what hit 'em."

We had only about twenty-five minutes to play, and the rule was that as soon as the first bell rang to call us back inside, the game was automatically over. It was always a pretty informal game. We didn't even have a jump ball, and of course no referee. Weeks ago we had flipped a coin to see who got the ball first, and we'd been trading off ever since.

It was their turn to start with the ball, so we jogged downcourt and settled into a two-one-two zone defense. Ryan and I were out front with Cory in the middle and Nat and Jimmy low.

A good-shooting, dark-haired kid named Mike Ancona brought the ball up and tried moving it in toward the bucket. His teammates kept passing the ball back out to him, so he finally drove the lane, switched hands on his way up, and scored.

"I could have stopped him," Ryan whispered to me on the way back upcourt.

I smiled at him as I dribbled. "Really? I've never been able to. Switch next time if you want to."

I was shaking my head. I wasn't offended that Ryan thought he could stop a guy who had shot over me. I liked his self-confidence and wondered what he had seen in Ancona's play that made him think he could be stopped.

I pulled up, faked a pass to Cory in the lane, then tossed the ball over Ancona's head to Ryan. As usual, Ryan was alert and had a plan. As Ancona's feet hit the floor, and before he had time to adjust, Ryan ignored his open shot and lofted the ball back to me.

Ancona was so sure that Ryan would take the easy shot that he scrambled to get back into position to leap and block it. But by the time he had done that, I had the ball, Ryan was empty-handed, Ancona was out of position, and I launched a shot. I was so eager to drill one off him that I put too much on the shot and it bounded high off the rim.

11

I followed the shot, not really expecting to get a rebound but hoping that someone on our team might. I wanted to be in position to help out.

Ryan, who somehow has a sixth sense about such things, bounded downcourt the other way. Sure enough, he had guessed right. Mike Ancona had recovered quickly from his defensive lapse and was headed that way ahead of everybody. His teammate grabbed the rebound and fired it ahead of him on one bounce toward the basket.

Ryan caught Mike and stayed with him step for step. Ancona gathered in the ball, had room and time for two dribbles and a shot, and took his first dribble. On the second, Ryan shot a hand in, stole the ball, and fired a pass the length of the court to the only player who was still at the other end: me.

Would you believe I blew that shot too? I guess I do better with the opposition hanging all over me. I missed the lay-up, missed the tip-in, and finally regrouped and scored.

As I jogged back, I could see Mike Ancona pointing at Ryan and hissing something about regretting "that." Ryan had to have heard him, but he didn't see Mike pointing, because his back was turned.

Ryan ignored him, and I could see a smile playing at the corner of Ryan's mouth. He wasn't the type to intentionally hassle someone, but he enjoyed playing the game correctly, and if that got somebody riled, that just meant you'd probably beat them too.

As usual in this kind of a game, the teams traded several turnovers and missed shots with neither team scoring for about five minutes.

I asked Ryan if he was ready to play point guard. He had shed his jacket and unbuttoned the top three buttons of his shirt. He was sweating and panting. He shook his head. "Just let me play Ancona one-on-one on defense."

I shrugged. Why not? We could stay in our basic zone and help out, letting Ryan stay with Ancona. It worked perfectly. The next two times Mike brought the ball downcourt, Ryan flashed in and stole it as clean as ever. Both times Ryan led a fast break back upcourt for the score, the first time dropping in the lay-up himself and the second time dishing off a pass to Jimmy for an easy basket.

Mike was getting madder and madder, and it affected his game. Of course, I didn't want to get him riled just for the fun of it, but if you can get a good player distracted and rattled, it can help you win. I watched to make sure Ryan wasn't rubbing it in or being a bad sport when he stole the ball. And he wasn't.

The next time down the court, Mike angrily dribbled the ball. He was always a high dribbler, but in his anger he was really banging it off the asphalt. A couple of times I was tempted to call him for carrying the ball, but without a ref that kind of thing always leads to arguments.

Ryan is a master ball-stealer. He played Mike loose and at one point pretended to have a lapse in concentration. That gave the boiling Ancona a false feeling that he had time to scope out which of his teammates was most open for a pass. As he scanned the floor, Ryan flashed in to steal the ball once more, mid-dribble.

As he started up court, with us leading by two baskets, Ancona took a wild swipe at the ball and smacked Ryan on the arm loud enough to be heard all over the playground. The ball bounced out of bounds.

"Our ball," Mike shouted.

"What do you mean, your ball?" Ryan squealed. "You fouled me, and it was out on you."

"Out on *you!*" Mike shrieked. "You little punk!"

Mike had the ball and stood just off the court with it over his head, ready to throw it in to his teammates. Even they knew his claim was ridiculous. "C'mon, Mike," one of them said. "It's their ball!"

"Whose side are you on?" Mike demanded.

"The logical side," Ryan said quietly, and that really set Mike off.

He slammed the ball to the ground, and it bounded way over all of our heads.

A teammate caught it and held it under his arm. "We haven't got much time, Mike, and we're gonna lose this game if we don't get goin' here."

"We're gonna lose anyway," Mike said, grabbing the ball. "This guy's cheatin'."

I wanted to argue with him, but it wasn't my fight.

Ryan said, "I don't have to cheat to steal the ball from you. But if you're going to be a big baby about it, go ahead and take the ball."

With that, Mike fired the ball at Ryan, and only Ryan's lightning reflexes kept him from taking it full in the face. It bounced off his ear, and when he fell to the ground, clutching his head, Mike jumped on him.

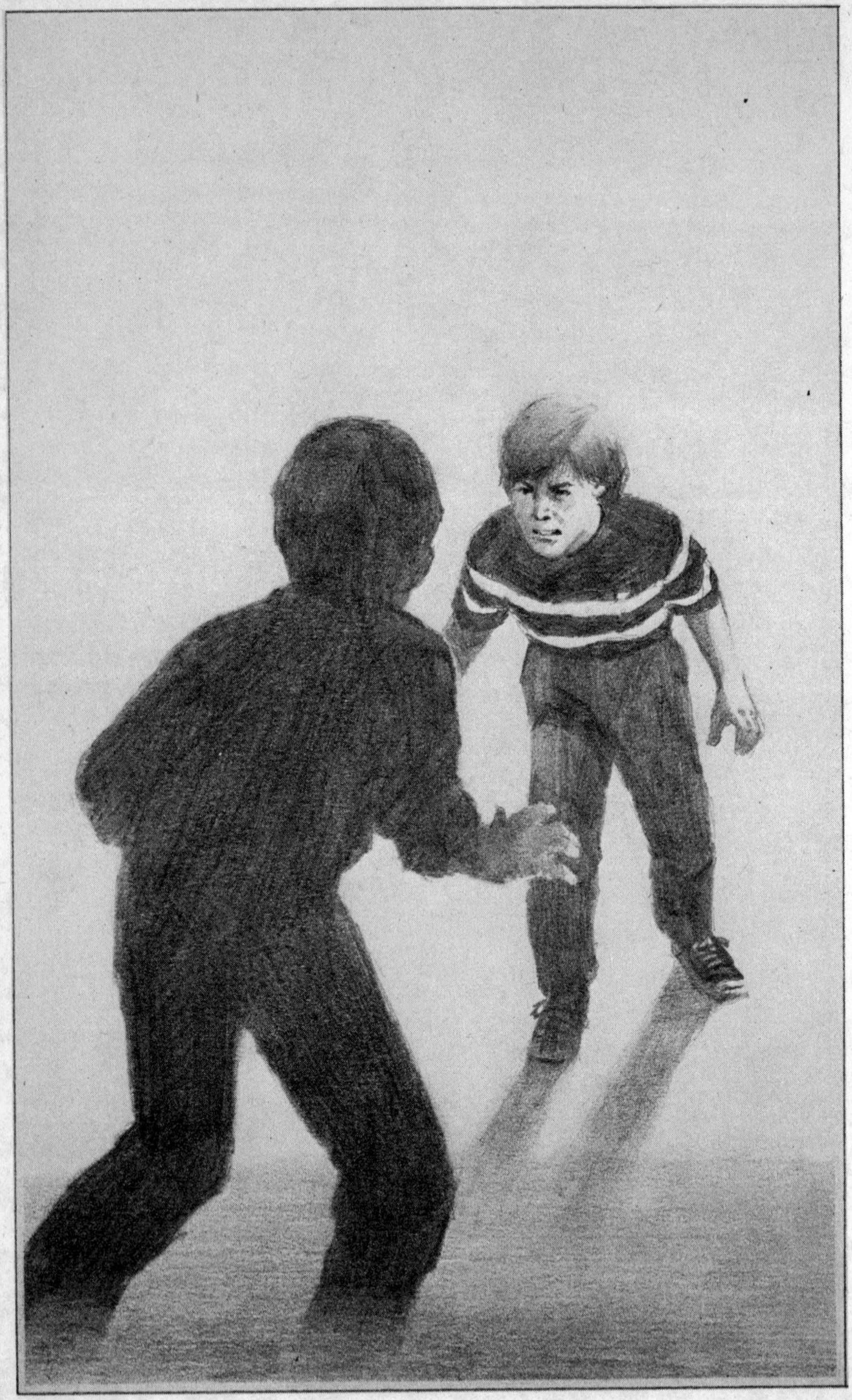

2

Defending Ryan

I might have let Ryan try to defend himself against the bigger Mike Ancona, but when Mike jumped him, Ryan was on his stomach, holding his head. He couldn't fight back in that position, and Mike began banging on the back of his head.

I looked at Mike's teammates, who knew Mike was wrong, but they just stood and watched and tried to form a wall so no teacher could see that a fight had started. Within seconds, dozens of kids from all over the playground had gathered to see what was going on.

Ryan flipped over and grabbed Mike by the neck, but now Ryan was on his back with a bigger kid on top of him. I knew that as soon as Ryan lost his grip, he would be beaten badly. Mike shifted his weight and got his knees up onto Ryan's shoulders, then lurched back to free his own arms and pulled his right fist back for a punch.

I stepped in and planted my thigh next to Mike's face, so that when he swung he wrapped his arm around my leg. I twisted my hips, pulling Mike off Ryan and slinging him to the ground. He rolled twice and leaped to his feet, coming straight for me. Lucky for me, my dad had been in special weapons and tactics in the Marines, so I knew how to defend myself.

My dad always told me that the easiest person to fight is one who is mad, because you can turn his anger against him. Ryan had already done that to Mike in the basketball game, and now I would have the chance as he charged me.

He was swinging wildly as I skipped backward. Kids were yelling and, I hoped, drawing teachers from the school. For two reasons I really didn't want to fight Mike. I didn't want to fight anybody, because I had a reputation as a good kid, smart enough, and a good sport. Anybody who knew me had to know I hadn't started this.

And also I had told many of the kids in the school about God. How would it look if the guy who claimed to be a Christian was beating up on somebody? I wanted to be sure that, by the time the teachers showed up, it would be obvious that I was just trying to keep from getting hurt and wasn't trying to hurt Mike. Others could defend me, those who knew I was just sticking up for Ryan.

Mike was quickly upon me, but I kept him at arms' length, trying to talk him down. "C'mon, Mike. You don't want to do this. Let's not fight. Cool down, and we can finish the game."

But he was crying and flailing. Somehow I was able to get hold of his wrists. That frustrated him to death. I've held the wrists of smaller kids before, and that usually stops them. When he didn't relax, I knew what was coming next. He pulled his foot back to kick me, and I didn't even want to try to guess where.

I couldn't let him do that. Just about anywhere a big twelve-year-old kicks you can hurt you. As soon as I saw him draw that foot back, I planted my feet and fell back, still hanging onto his wrists. With all my weight I yanked on his arms, and with him up on one foot, he was completely off balance.

I fell on my back, and he went tumbling over me. I let go to keep from breaking his arms, and he slid across the grass at the edge of the blacktop court. Now he was really mad, and he jumped up swinging. I didn't want to hit him; I really didn't. When he missed with two roundhouse swings, one with each arm, I could have popped him in the chest or the face each time. But I didn't.

I was so glad that that was what everybody saw. They had been yelling for me to "Smack him, Dallas! Get him!" But I just didn't want to. For one thing, it would have been too easy. My dad showed me how to take a guy who was raging, and once he proved it when I got mad. He didn't hurt me, but he showed me how easy it was to defend yourself against somebody like that.

Now, as Mike came screaming at me again, I just kept dancing back and slapping at his hands. He left me so many openings to drill him one or two in the mouth that I was almost sorry I had decided not to hit him.

I glanced up to see if any teachers were there yet. I couldn't wait for them to break it up. While I was distracted, Mike got in a punch that grazed my ear. Man, did that hurt! It almost made me mad enough to hit him back, but no teachers were around, and I didn't want it to turn into something uglier than it already was.

I grabbed his wrists again, and I sensed him tensing to try to kick me again. But even in his rage, his memory was good. He didn't want to go flying again. While he hesitated I skipped around behind him, losing hold of one of his wrists while doing it. I wrapped him in a big bear hug and lifted my feet off the ground.

He was like a wild bull. We were pretty much the same size, though I was maybe an inch taller. Now he was carrying twice his normal weight, and he couldn't reach me to do anything about it. He tried to kick me in the shins by driving his heel back, but then he was trying to carry all that weight on one foot, and he tumbled to the ground.

Neither of us realized that we had maneuvered back to the blacktop again, and when he went down—with me on top of him—his knees and elbows ground into the asphalt. He struggled to get up, but I could tell he hadn't given up yet. He wasn't just going to check on his wounds. He was ready to fight. So I stayed where I was.

I planted my knees in his back and sat on him, not letting him bend his knees to get any leverage. "I'm staying here until you've had enough," I told him. And I heard the bell ring.

Some of the kids started moving toward the building, and it was then that I heard someone say, "Coach Schultz!" and everyone went running, even Mike Ancona's teammates.

I nodded to my friends to go back in too, but Ryan insisted on staying.

Coach Schultz, a big, heavy man, lumbered up. "O'Neil! Git off him! What do you think you're doin'?"

Just before the coach grabbed me, I slid off.

"What's goin' on here?"

"He jumped me!" Mike said, crying. His elbows were bleeding, and he rubbed his knees.

Coach Schultz knows us both, and he knew I wouldn't jump anybody without a reason. "Why?"

"I don't know!" Mike said.

"Why, Dallas?" the coach said.

"He knows," I said.

"Well, somebody tell me, or you're both gonna be in big trouble!"

Ryan spoke up. "Mike was beating me up, and Dallas was protecting me. That's all."

"Is it all over?" the coach said.

The three of us nodded.

"Then I want you all to shake hands."

I stuck my hand out.

Mike took it slowly and didn't squeeze it at all.

"I hope I didn't hurt you," I said. "I didn't mean to."

"Oh, sure," he said. "You just threw me down on the blacktop."

"Now is it all over or not?" Coach Schultz demanded.

"It's all over," Mike muttered.

Ryan reached to shake his hand, and, from how slowly he reacted, I was sure Mike shook just as unenthusiastically as he had with me. He whispered something to Ryan that made Ryan turn white.

"Now don't be makin' any threats!" the coach said. "It's s'posed to be all over. You get back at this kid and you'll answer to me!"

"I didn't say nothin'," Mike muttered.

As we walked back into the building, Coach Schultz asked me for the details of the fight.

I told him what had happened.

"Just tempers then, huh?" he asked.

"I think so," I said. "It won't happen again."

But when Mike ran on to his class, Ryan caught up with me. He was nearly in tears. "Oh, man," he said. "I'm really in trouble now."

"What do you mean? Coach Schultz is not going to report it. He knows it was just tempers flaring."

"I wish he *would* report it!"

"Why, Ry?"

"So when I get beat up, everybody will know who's responsible!"

"You're not going to get beat up!"

"Yes, I am! Mike guaranteed that!"

"He'll be in trouble with the coach!"

"Mike's not gonna do it himself."

"Who's gonna do it?"

"He told me he was going to get Gabriel Irving after me."

I stopped. "Gabriel Irving?"

"Yeah. Even you're afraid of him!"

"Well, he's a pretty tough kid," I said, laughing nervously. "But he's not gonna beat you up just because Mike Ancona tells him to."

"I hope you're right, but I'm not taking any chances."

The second bell rang, and we each had a minute to get to our classes. "What are you going to do?" I asked.

21

"I'm going to set my locker combination so all I have to do is give it one twist to the right and then I can be the first one out of the school. I'll be home before the junior high even lets out."

The junior high, where the well-known bully Gabriel Irving was a sixteen-year-old eighth-grader, was a block away. Our school let out ten minutes ahead of theirs so that just this kind of a problem wouldn't happen. Mixing those age groups was always trouble, so they told us.

"You don't have any beef with Gabriel," I said. "If he tries to bother you, just tell him that you thought Mike Ancona could take care of himself, especially against someone as small as you."

"In other words, you want me to tell him to pick on somebody his own size?"

"Yeah."

"*You* want to tell him that, Dallas?"

"Not particularly."

"Neither do I."

The late bell was ringing, and we ran off in different directions.

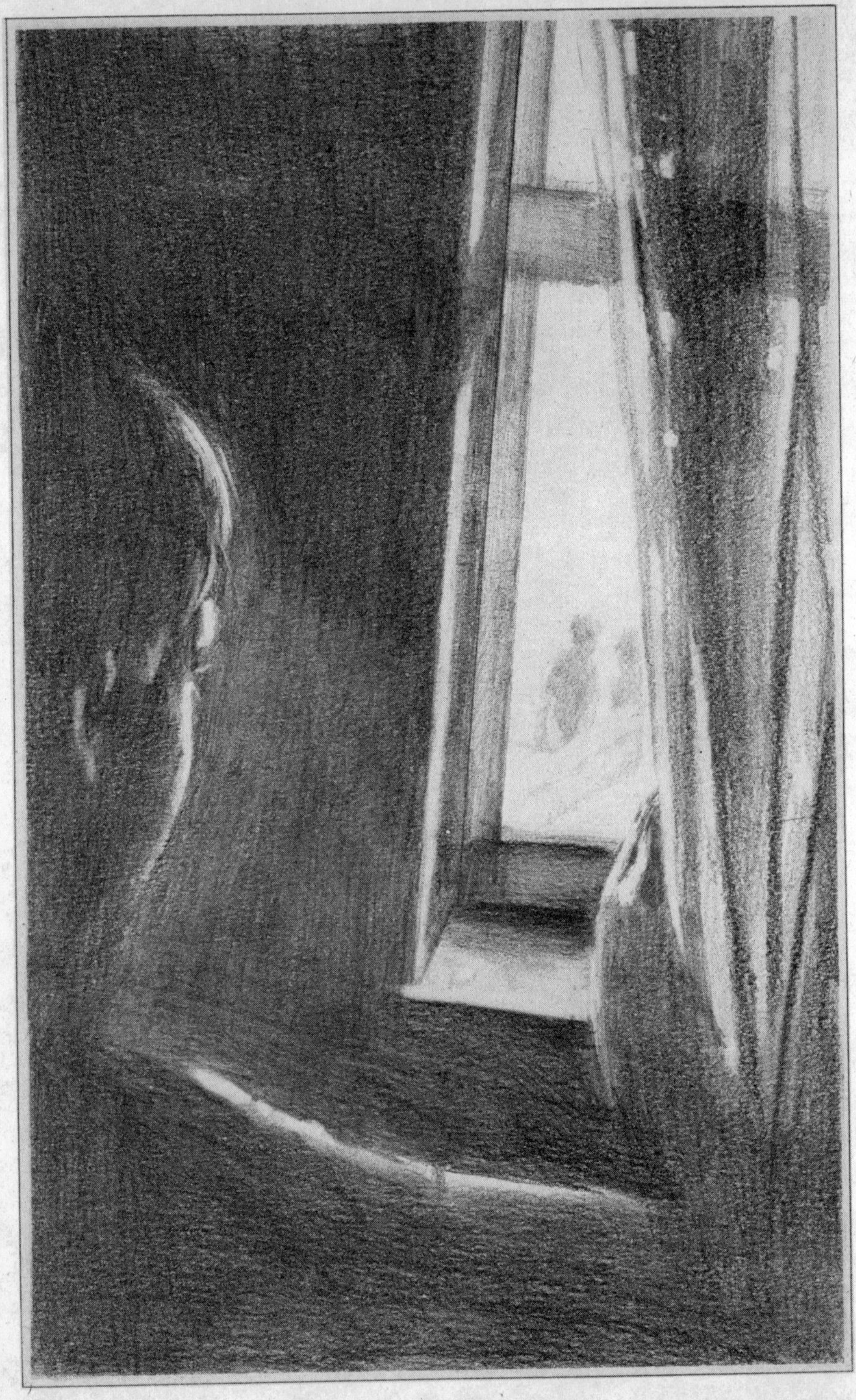

3

Fear

I couldn't imagine what Ryan was going through that day. He had to run past both sixth grade classrooms to get to his locker. I saw him, but he didn't see me. I know he had his eyes and his mind on getting in and out of his locker before Mike saw him and remembered his threat.

If Ryan had thought about it, he would have realized that there was no way Mike could get to Gabriel before the junior high let out, so Ryan really had nothing to worry about that day. But maybe he was worried that Mike would attack him again.

I thought Ryan could take Mike if he had to, but I never suggested fighting if there was any other way to settle something. And there usually was.

Jimmy and I strolled to our bikes after school and ran into Mike. "Hey, Ancona, why don't you lay off of Ryan, huh?" Jimmy suggested. "Let bygones be bygones."

"Forget it, Calabresi," Mike said. "He plays like that, he has to answer to me."

"He could answer to you easy enough," Jimmy said. "But he shouldn't have to worry about some overgrown eighth grader."

I cringed. I had told Jimmy what Ryan had told me, but I had forgotten to tell him not to say anything. Obviously, Mike had whispered that threat to Ryan and didn't expect him to tell Coach Schultz or me. Here three hours or so had passed and even Jimmy knew all about it.

"Oh," Mike said, "so the little baby has already been crying about it? Good. That's perfect. Now I'll be sure not to disappoint him."

Mike started to run off toward the junior high. "Hey, Ancona!" Jimmy called after him. "You can't even handle a fifth grader by yourself?"

Ancona walked back and put his face near Jimmy's. "I was handlin' him pretty good by myself today, wasn't I? Until your friend butted in."

"So you can't take someone your own size either?" Jimmy said, laughing.

"You're gonna get it too, Calabresi," Mike said. "Just watch your mouth."

"Ooh, I'm scared," Jimmy said, waving him off.

When Mike was gone, I suggested that we ride to Ryan's and make sure he got home all right.

"What do you mean, got home all right? He's not expecting trouble until tomorrow, is he?"

"He sure lit out of here a little while ago," I said. "Let's check on him."

"What time's basketball practice?"

"After dinner—in Ferguson's shed," I said.

"I hate that place."

"We all do. Inconsistent bounce, plywood floors, hardly any light. But it sure makes us good when we get on a real court."

Jimmy couldn't argue with that. "I guess we've got time to see Ryan."

Ryan always got home an hour before his mother did, but when we got there it was hard to tell anyone was there. The basketball hoop on the garage was unused. His bike was nowhere to be seen. The shades were down, the drapes pulled, the door shut. From what we could tell, there wasn't a light on in the place.

"Maybe he rode to his aunt's," Jimmy said. "She's only a few blocks away."

I looked in the side door of the garage. It was locked, but his bike was in there. "He wouldn't have walked if he was worried about someone out looking for him," I said. "He must be home."

We rang the bell. No answer, but I thought I heard movement in the house. "Watch the front curtains," I said. "I'll watch the window in the front door."

I rang it again.

"I saw the curtain move!" Jimmy said.

I shushed him. "Then he's peeked out and knows it's us."

The door opened a crack. "Put your bikes in the back, and then you can come in," Ryan said hurriedly.

"C'mon!" I said. "Just let us in. If anybody comes after you, they'll see our bikes and know we're here. Anyway, what makes you think they have any idea where you live?"

He let us in, and we all sat in the dark living room.

"Man," Jimmy said, "you've got it bad."

"Wouldn't you?"

Jimmy shook his head. "Nah. Not afraid of Ancona. Anyway, you're not gonna fight him, right? Just tell him you're real sorry, you didn't mean to show him up or make it look like you were cheatin', or whatever you were supposed to have done, and ask him if you can still be friends."

"We never *were* friends," Ryan said. "I hardly even knew who he was until I played against him today. I knew he had a high dribble. I noticed that before when I watched you guys play. He's pretty good, Dallas, but you should have been able to steal the ball from him before, just like I did today."

I shrugged. For a little kid so afraid of someone beating up on him, he sure wasn't afraid to speak his mind.

We talked to him until his mother got home, and then he seemed to get bolder. "You guys want to shoot some baskets?"

"You sure the bogey man isn't out there waiting for you?" I teased.

"C'mon, Dallas! It's not funny. You know I'm not going to be able to come to practice tonight."

"Why not?"

"Forget it. No way."

"Why not?"

"Because I won't want to be out riding around after dark by myself."

"You've been doing it for weeks!"

"Well, I won't be doing it again for a long time."

"You'd better be kidding," I said.

"I'm not. If I have to drop off the team, I will."

"Don't even say that."

"I'm serious, Dallas. I'm not going to let those guys get me."

Jimmy broke in. "Ryan, have you ever seen Gabriel Irving?"

"No, but I've heard enough about him."

"We all have, but even though he's sixteen and could probably shave already, he's just a runt. Strong and wiry, but puny."

"You think I could take him?" Ryan asked.

"No, but he's not going to hurt you."

"How about him *and* Mike?"

"That wouldn't be a fair fight," Jimmy said.

"What do they care about that?" Ryan said.

I stood. "Well, if you're really not coming to practice—"

"I'm not."

"—then we'd better shoot a little here. Did you know that you've almost cracked the starting five, and I was going to tell you soon that I thought you'd be starting within a couple of weeks?"

"You're serious?"

28

I nodded.

"Who's he beating out?" Jimmy asked with a pained look.

"Who knows?" I said. "Maybe you."

"No way," Jimmy said, but he wasn't so sure, and it showed.

We went out and shot baskets, but Jimmy was thinking about losing his starting job, and Ryan was always looking out into the street to see if he had any intruders. We weren't doing well or getting much done.

"We'd better call it quits," I said. "Jimmy and I need to save some energy for practice, and he'd better do better in the shed than he did here, or I'll be able to make my decision tonight."

"No way," Jimmy said again. "I gotta get goin' if I'm gonna have dinner before practice."

"Do me a favor, will ya, Jim?" I said. "Call my mom, and tell her I'll be home in about a half hour. I've got to talk to Ryan a little."

Jimmy nodded and rode off.

"I'm not coming tonight, and that's final," Ryan said.

"Suit yourself," I said. "But we still need to talk." We sat on the driveway with our backs up against the cold garage door.

"Listen, I know what you must be going through."

"I doubt it. You didn't look like you were afraid of anything today when you were fighting Mike."

"First of all, I wasn't fighting him. If you remember, I just got him off you and held him off for a while."

"You were on top of him, Dallas!"

"I had to be. It was the only way to keep him from hitting me again. And I *was* scared!"

"Yeah? So how come he didn't threaten you and promise to sic Gabriel Irving on you?"

I shrugged. "Probably because he knows that he can't always have Gabriel with him when I'm around. And he saw that I wasn't afraid of him and that I could take him if I had to."

"So you *weren't* afraid of him!"

"I was afraid of the mess I was getting into, and, yes, I was afraid that he might be able to take me. I don't think he can now, but part of the reason is that I hid my fear from him. He doesn't think I'm at all afraid of him, and that's exactly what I want him to think."

Ryan sat silent. He shook his head. "I can't get away with that. He was beatin' on me, and I *am* afraid of him."

"He must be a little afraid of you too, don't you think?"

"No, I don't think! Why would you say that?"

"Why is he siccing Gabriel on you, then? He must not think he can handle you himself. He must worry a little about a guy who's a good enough athlete to make him look bad. I think he wonders if he could really take you in a fair fight, so he has to have protection."

"You're forgetting something," Ryan said. "He knows you're around to protect me at school. That's the only reason he's bringing in someone to back him up."

"Well, I have some strategy for you tomorrow anyway. And if it works, you'll scare him away from threatening you, trying to take you himself, and even siccing Gabriel on you."

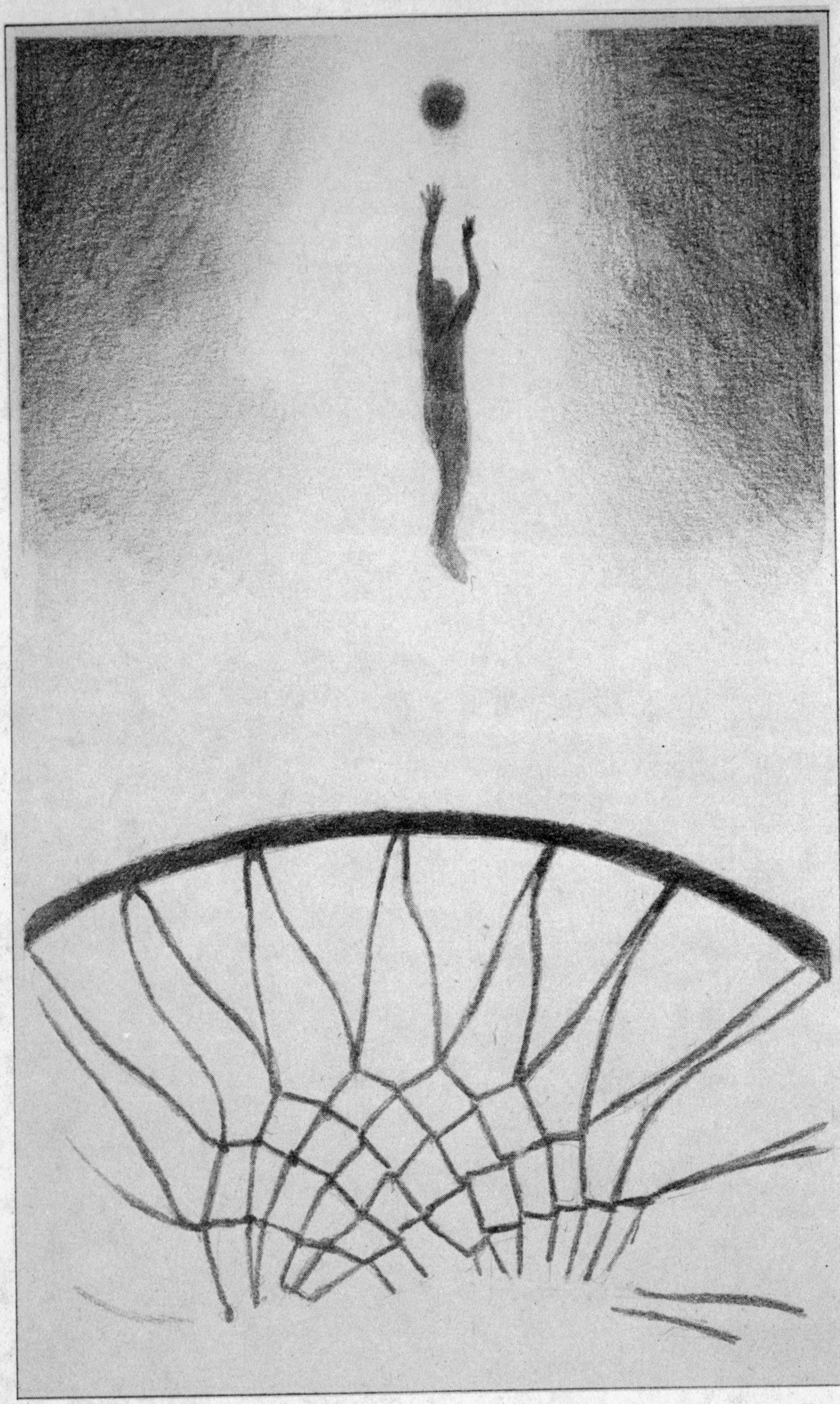

4

The Strategy

My plan was simple, but I was convinced it would work. "When you see Mike Ancona at school tomorrow," I said, "compliment him."

"On what?"

"His basketball ability. His personality. Anything."

"His *personality!?*"

"I mean before yesterday. You never had any reason to think he was such a—"

"I know! In fact, I thought he was a pretty cool guy, a good basketball player."

"Tell him that!" I said. "That's exactly what I mean."

"What's the point? He hates me. He's after me. He's siccing Gabriel Irving on me. I don't like him. I don't want to compliment him on anything."

"It was just a thought."

"You still haven't told me what good it's supposed to do."

"The Bible says that if you treat your enemy kindly it's like heaping coals of fire on his head."

"I wouldn't mind doing *that!*"

"Then find something good you can say about him, and say it to him. Tell him you like him and that no matter what he does or says to you, it won't change the fact that you like him."

"I don't know if I can do that, Dal."

"Try it. What have you got to lose?"

That night at practice we ran through all the drills we could manage in the little loft court. The five starters stayed after everyone else had gone home. We liked to occasionally practice running through our plays without any opposition. It was not only fun, but it was also good for us. We glided up and down the court, passing hard and crisp to each other, never breaking stride, always finding the open man—because everyone was always open.

Jimmy and Jack especially liked this kind of practice. Bugsy was best at it, looking so fast it was scary.

Cory was the one who didn't see any sense in it. "We'll never have it this good in a game, man!" he'd say.

"Then enjoy it while it lasts," Jimmy said, firing a bounce pass to Jack underneath.

Practicing that way made me want to play a game right then. During the basketball season, I couldn't get enough of the game. I had played at lunchtime, at Ryan's, and in the loft. And when Jimmy and I rode home, he stopped at my place, and we shot a few hoops there too.

"Are you really gonna replace me with Ryan in the starting five?"

"Did I say that?"

"You might as well have. I know I'm the weak link."

"I wouldn't say that."

"You don't have to. You're too nice. All you have to do is replace me, and I'll get the message."

"Our starting five is gonna be awfully hard to break into," I said. "Ryan knows that."

"Yeah, but I saw him play today. He made Mike Ancona look sick, and that kid can play."

34

"I know. He's gonna start for the Condors this year."

"Really? Jack's old team?"

I nodded. "And taking the place of the coach's son, who moved up to the older league, takes some kind of a ballplayer."

What happened next showed the difference between Jimmy and me, and maybe the reason I was willing to defend my friends, even when I was afraid of bullies. Of course, I didn't think about that at the time.

Jimmy stood left of the basket where the corner would be on a regulation court. I stood under the basket and lazily bounced passes to him after every shot. He got into a rhythm and bagged six in a row.

"You're on a roll," I said. "Wanna see how many you can make out of twenty?"

"Bet I can't make ten," he said.

"Are you kidding? Jimmy! You're six for six now! Go for it!"

He shrugged and signaled for the ball. He made two more, the second bouncing around the rim and skimming the backboard before dropping through. He shook his head. "Slop shot," he said. "I'm losing it."

"Time out," I said.

"What do you mean, time out? You said yourself I was on a roll. Don't get me out of my rhythm."

"Sit down, Jim," I said. "We have to talk."

He looked at his watch, and we sat in the gravel near his bike. "How am I gonna make any more if I don't shoot?" he said.

"Jimmy, listen, you know I don't like to come off like I'm an adult or your dad or anything, but I need to tell you that if I take you out of the starting lineup, it won't be because of your ability."

"I'm slow."

"I know, but you're big too."

"I'm not too accurate."

"You're the fourth highest scorer on the team."

35

"Out of five. Big deal."

"It's your attitude, Jimmy. You always expect the worst."

"I'm realistic," he said. "What's wrong with that?"

I stood and began casually dribbling and shooting.

Jimmy stayed where he was, looking at the ground. "Now what did I do?" he asked. "Make you mad?"

"You usually do."

"What's that supposed to mean?"

"You don't want any help. I'm not trying to be a know-it-all. I just see that you're down on yourself, always thinking negatively. Why don't you assume the best, work hard, play hard, practice hard, get the most out of yourself?"

"Thanks, coach."

"All right, then. Just forget it."

"You mad at me?"

"Course. Why shouldn't I be?"

"You don't like me anymore?"

"Of course I do, Jim. See? You always assume the worst. Can't I be mad at you without dropping you as a friend? Listen to me for a second, will you?"

"All right, I'm listening."

"Get back up here in position to shoot, and don't tell yourself that you've lost it just because your last shot was a little sloppy. Tell yourself you were lucky, but that you made your own luck by shooting so well. Tell yourself that you're still eight for eight and that you're going to get right back into the groove. No, you're not going to make all twenty. My dad and I hold the record out here with seventeen."

"I thought you said nineteen!"

"That was from the free-throw line. That's an easier shot. You're shooting from the baseline where you almost have to swish it. But just tell yourself you're going to make all the rest. And then do it. If you miss one, so what? Keep going. Get back in the groove. Think ahead, not behind."

Jim stood and stretched. "Ooh, I'm sore from practice," he said.

"Another excuse," I said.

"Give me a break, Dal! Don't make me quit complainin' too! It's about the only thing I enjoy doing as much as hasslin' you."

I laughed and tossed him the ball.

He dribbled back to his spot on the baseline in the imaginary corner. He launched a shot with a perfect motion, but the ball hit the far side of the rim and bounced back to him. "See?" he said.

"Listen to yourself!" I said. "You know as well as I do that you missed that shot by only a quarter of an inch. And you're eight for nine! Think of it! Eight for nine! Don't remind yourself that you just made your first miss. Tell yourself that you're on the way to a record. You only missed one by a tiny bit, and you can get right back in the groove. That shot was so close that you shouldn't even have to adjust your shot. Shoot it the same way again, and it'll probably drop right through."

"I'm supposed to think ahead?"

"Right."

"All I can think of is that I have to make nine more just to tie the record."

"Jimmy! You've got eleven more shots! You went eight for nine; you can go nine for eleven."

"Yeah, but if I go nine for the *first* eleven, then I have to make all the rest."

"Jimmy! Good grief! You're talking yourself out of it already! If you go nine for eleven, you have only nine shots left. You made your first eight and barely missed the ninth. Why couldn't you make nine in a row?"

"Because I'm not that good."

I shrugged and shook my head. "You're only as good as you think you are," I said. "Where did you get this attitude?"

He muttered something about being realistic.

"Just hurry up and get it over with," I added. "I gotta go in."

He could see that I was really angry now, so he sheepishly dribbled a couple of times and set himself to shoot. His next three shots were swishers, nothing but net. I could see him fighting a smile.

"Don't fight it," I said. "You can do it. You can break the record. Tell yourself you can, and you will."

He shook his head, but he was smiling. I could tell he liked my encouraging him, and I think he was also glad that I was no longer mad. His next shot hit the far side of the rim, bounced high, hit the near side, and dropped through. "I don't want to lose it now," he said.

"*Lose* it?" I said. "Everything's going your way. You can't miss! Even when you're a little off, your shots are dropping. So get back in the groove. Make the rest. Every one!"

"Twelve for thirteen," he whispered to himself, taking aim. His shot was an airball, hitting nothing. I scrambled to get it and fire it back to him.

"OK," I said. "No problem. You got the bad shot out of your system. Don't let it bother you. Forget the twelve for fourteen. Think of the next six. That's all you need to worry about. You made eight in a row and four in a row. Now if you can make six in a row, the record is yours."

He started to shake his head, but I glared at him in the harsh light from the side of the garage. His next shot rattled in the rim and went through. Thirteen for fifteen. A swisher. Fourteen for sixteen. A roll-around-the-rimmer that seemed to never quit till it fell through. Fifteen for seventeen.

The next shot hit the near side of the rim and skipped over and into the net. "Sixteen for eighteen!" Jimmy yelled. "I don't believe it!"

"Why not? You did it! You're the only one shooting. Give yourself some credit, man. It's you. Nobody else."

"All I have to do is to make one of the last two to tie you and your dad."

"Wrong attitude."

"Why?!"

"What are you worried about tying for? You hit eight in a row, four in a row, and four in a row. Two in a row should be easy."

"But that would make six in a row!"

"Forget that! Nothing else matters but these two. Just two. Make 'em!"

Jimmy stood in position and dribbled. He set the ball near his chest, then over his head with both hands. He stopped and took a deep breath, then laughed nervously. "I can't even remember how to shoot," he said. "And it's not a bad attitude, Dallas. I really can't remember if I shoot from here, or here."

He had held the ball low and then high.

"I know the feeling," I said. "Happens to me all the time. Just back off the line, dribble a couple of times, step up and shoot without thinking about it. It'll go through."

"I hope so," he said.

"That's the difference," I reminded him. "I know so."

"You know I'm going to make it?"

"Absolutely."

He turned his back to the basket and took a deep breath. He dribbled twice, turned around, set himself, and swished it. Seventeen for nineteen.

"No way I'm breakin' your record," Jimmy said.

"Jimmy! You're hopeless!"

He stepped up to shoot again.

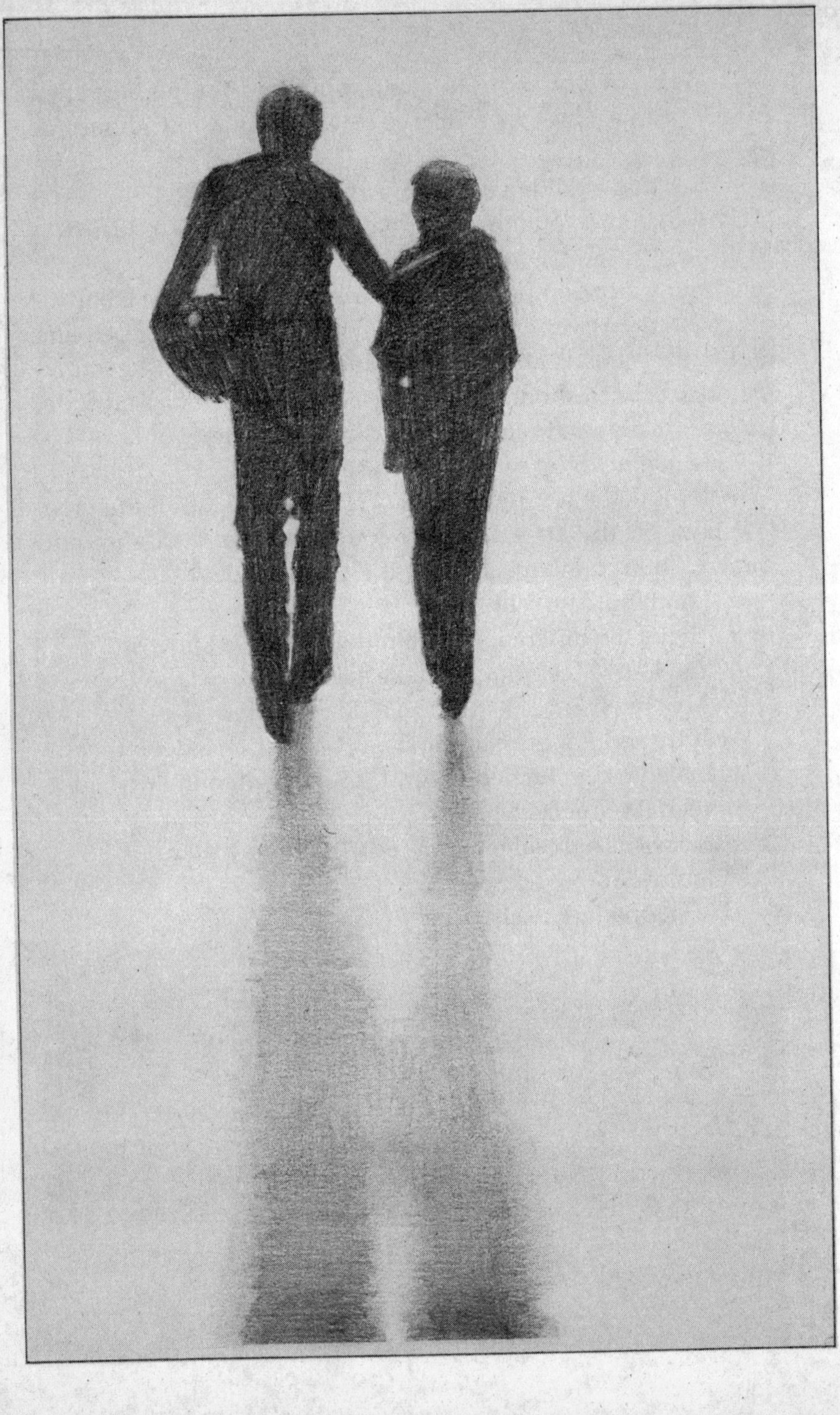

5

The Record

Jimmy dribbled the ball with both hands, then set it between his feet. He was bent over, but he turned his face up to look at me. He gritted his teeth in a huge grin and rubbed his hands together. "I don't believe how bad I want to make this shot," he said. He danced around laughing while the ball rolled away. "Ooh, I can't stand it!"

"You're going to talk yourself right out of it," I said.

"It's just one shot. Simple. Don't think about the record now. Just think about the shot."

"That's easy for you to say," he said. "You don't have to shoot it."

"You want me to shoot it for you? I can make one shot any time I want."

"Sure!" he said.

I figured I had nothing to lose. If I missed, we'd both laugh, and if I made it he'd still insist on breaking the record— or at least trying to—all on his own. I nonchalantly picked up the ball, slid into position, and fired through a perfect shot. "See?" I said. "Nothing to it." Of course, there had been no pressure on me.

"You'd better just step up and shoot it, Jim," I said. "Don't talk yourself out of it. That's what coaches try to do when they call time just before an opponent's important free throw. They give him time to think about it and lose confidence."

"I'm definitely losing confidence," Jimmy said. "Give me the ball."

"Just tell yourself you're going to make it, and take the shot," I encouraged.

Jimmy got in position and called for the ball. I bounced it to him.

I could see on his face that he was tight as a drum. He readied himself to shoot. As soon as he let the shot go, I knew he had hesitated, let up, hadn't followed through. The ball was dead in the air, heading straight for the near side of the rim.

I feared it would hit it so straight on that it would bounce down or back to Jimmy, but it hit just high enough to bounce up. We stood staring as if it were in slow motion. The ball went up, came down on the near side of the rim, bounced to the far side, then hit on the back and rolled off the front. No good.

Jimmy pretended to be mad, kicking and shouting, but I could tell he was thrilled to have come so close and to have tied my dad and me for the record. "Beat *that*, turkey!" he crowed.

"You know what?" I said.

"What?"

"That gives me confidence. It doesn't bother me that you tied me. I was hoping you'd *break* the record."

"Oh, sure."

".I *was*! That would convince me that if you could do it, I could break it."

I hadn't meant that to sound like it sounded, but Jimmy understood it full force and he was offended. "Thanks a lot, Dallas."

"I didn't mean it that way. I was just trying to show you a positive way to look at things."

"Right. You figure if your jerky friend can hit seventeen out of twenty, you have to be able to hit at least eighteen."

"I didn't mean it that way. I'm sorry, Jimmy. Really. I didn't mean that. Forgive me?"

He pressed his lips together and nodded. He always hated when I apologized because then he had to forgive me, even if he didn't want to. He was so shy about talking that way that he hardly ever said he was sorry or asked forgiveness. "I gotta get goin'," he said, moving toward his bike.

"You mean I don't get a chance to shoot?" I said.

"Shoot all you want."

"I need a rebounder."

"Get your own rebounds," he said.

"That's not fair," I said. "We always rebound for each other. You're not supposed to be able to shoot unless you've rebounded."

He sighed loudly and stood under the basket. My first four shots were swishers that bounced right back to me. The next went through the hoop but came straight down toward Jimmy and bounced away. He ran after it and threw a long pass to me that made me move to catch it.

"C'mon!" I complained. "You're gonna throw off my rhythm."

"Poor baby," he said.

I couldn't believe he wasn't still thrilled with his seventeen baskets.

I hit four more swishers and was nine for nine when the outside light went on and off several times. That was my signal to come in, and right now. I shot one more and made it. I was ten for ten.

"Finish up," Jimmy urged. "They won't mind."

"Nah," I said. "I'd better get in."

"All right," he said a little too quickly. "See ya."

He hopped on his bike and rode off, glad—I was sure—that he didn't have to stick around and see me take a chance at the record.

I hurried inside and told my dad about Jimmy's shooting and that I was ten for ten. I begged him to let me finish.

"I'll rebound for you," he said. He came out in his construction boots and khaki pants, along with a sleeveless tee shirt. "Hoo boy, it's cold out here," he said. "How 'bout lettin' me shoot first?"

"Dad!" I scolded. "I'm ten for ten!"

"Oh, that's right! Rhythm and all that. Where you shootin' from?"

"The side."

"You're ten for ten from the side? That's got to be a record in itself."

"No, Dad. When you got your seventeen, you were three for five and six for nine. You hit the last eleven."

"I did? What a memory!"

I missed four shots in a row and slammed the ball to the ground. It bounced high over the roof and came down into Dad's hands.

"All right," he said. "You can't tie even your best, but sixteen for twenty is nothing to sneeze at. Make the last six for practice staying in the groove."

I wanted nothing more than to show him I could do it. And I did.

"Thanks, Dad," I said, tucking the ball under my arm and heading for the house.

"Hey, whoa, hold on a minute," he said. "Rebounder gets to shoot, doesn't he?"

"You want to shoot?"

"Course I do. What fun is it to come out here in the cold and rebound for a kid who can't hit the broad side of a barn?"

"Dad!"

He was grinning. I gave him the ball and got under the hoop. I never saw anything like it. He missed the first shot by a mile, made eighteen straight, and missed the last one. I accused him of doing it on purpose. "You could have made them all, couldn't you?" I said.

"No, sir. I tried my best on every shot. Now Dallas," he said, putting his arm on my shoulder as we went in, "I want you to do me a favor. You're gonna want to tell Jimmy about this tomorrow, aren't you?"

"Tomorrow?! Tonight!"

"Not tonight. And when you tell him tomorrow, I want you to do me a favor. Tell him that you came back out and tried to break the record and wound up with sixteen. Don't tell him what I did."

"Why not, Dad? You want me to lie to him? Make him think he still tied the record?"

"He still shares the record for kids, Dal. If he asks, you have to tell him, but otherwise let him enjoy his time in the sun, huh?"

"What does that mean?"

"His little time of glory. Let him enjoy sharing a record. He doesn't need to know his record was broken a few minutes after he tied it. Understand?"

I nodded. "You tried your best in breaking it, right, Dad?"

"Absolutely."

"Well, let me ask you something, then. If Jimmy had still been here, and you knew what he had done, would you have still tried your best and got eighteen?"

"What do you think?"

"I think you wouldn't have."

"You're exactly right."

"Then you haven't always tried your best to break the record you and I share."

"I didn't say that."

"You might as well have."

"No, I don't need to do that for you. You can take it if your records get broken. You have a lot of things going for you that Jimmy doesn't. Let's just let him enjoy this awhile, OK?"

I nodded. The next day Jimmy didn't even ask if I had been allowed to finish shooting. The talk around the school was that something was up between Ryan and Mike Ancona. I couldn't wait to find out what it was.

45

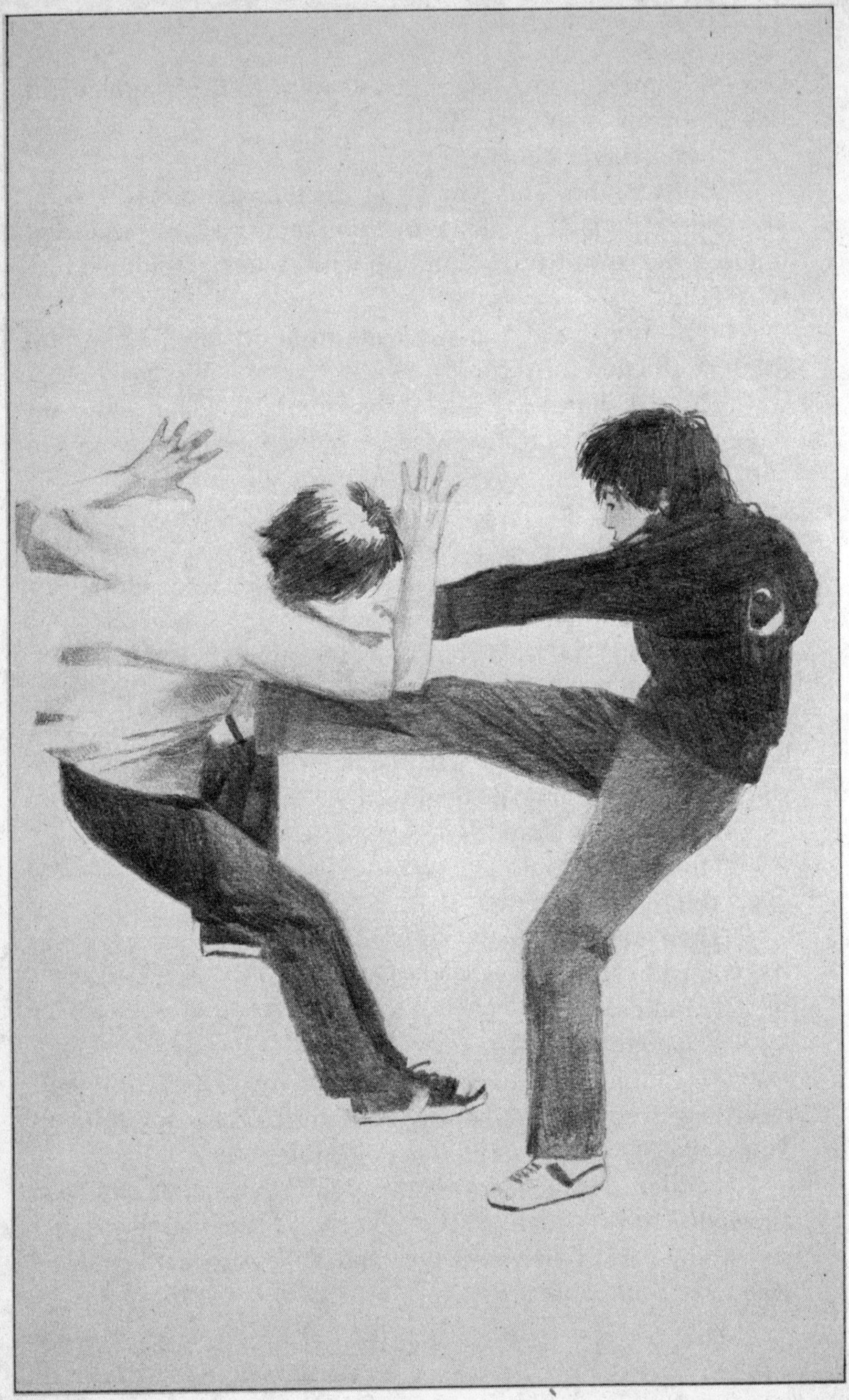

6

The Scare

A crowd had gathered out at the far end of the playground near the backstop. I ran as fast as I could, sliding in the dirt and pushing my way through to see what was going on. Ryan was standing there with his arms folded, refusing to take a step toward or away from Mike.

Mike taunted him. "What'sa matter, chicken?"

"I told you, Mike," Ryan said, his voice trembling. "I don't want to fight you. I want to be your friend. I like you. You're a good athlete and can be a nice guy."

With that, Mike charged Ryan, knocking him to the ground. So much for my advice. I looked back toward the school building. No teachers were aware of what was going on, which was good for Ryan. I didn't care if Mike got into trouble, because he deserved it, but Ryan was trying to avoid the fight.

I moved in and bent over Mike, who hadn't noticed me yet. "Let him up right now, or you'll regret it," I said quietly.

His body went limp, and he rolled off Ryan. "You again?" he said. "Can't this punk fight his own battles?"

"Can't you?" I asked. "Why should he be expected to fight somebody bigger if you can't? And remember, you're the one who threatened to bring Gabe Irving into it."

"Yeah, well, just wait and see. Gabriel will be in on it, and he's going to take you too."

"Listen, Mike, if you're gonna stay out of it, why don't both you and Ryan stay out of it? Just let it be Gabriel and me. How's that sound?"

"Forget it, man," Mike said, his face red as the crowd broke up. "Gabriel is after both of you, and I want to see it happen."

"When and where?" I asked, trying to sound braver than I was.

"In the alley after school, as soon as the junior high lets out. Everybody there knows about it, so there'll be lots of witnesses."

"That's OK with me," I said. "I'm not going to let anyone beat up on my friend. Too bad for you."

"Why too bad for me?"

"Because no matter what happens, even if I win the fight with Gabriel, if Ryan gets hurt I'm comin' after you. And you know what else? You can tell Gabriel for me that I think he's a sissy, a chicken, a wimp. I say he's too scared to face me one on one."

"You really want me to tell him that?"

"You bet I do. All you bullies are the same. You're nothing but talk and showing off, beatin' up kids smaller than you. Gabe and me, nobody else. Otherwise he's everything I said he was."

"You're crazy, man," Mike said. "Irving's gonna kill you." I feared he was right about my being crazy. I didn't really worry about getting killed. I had seen Gabriel Irving fight before. He fought dirty. Not that there's a good way to fight, but there's fair and there's cheating.

I once saw a crowd gathered around Gabriel while he was taunting a high school kid. I had to admit the high schooler was bigger, but he looked weak and out of shape, not hard and tough like Gabriel.

"What are the rules?" the big kid wanted to know, his lips quivering even as he tried to sound calm.

"Well, let's see," Gabriel said, talking softly and moving close to the older kid. "Let's say no kicking, like you can't do this." He turned sideways and lifted his leg, moving his foot close to the big kid's stomach. Then he bent his knee and kicked the kid as hard as he could. Everyone could hear the air burst from the kid's lungs.

As he fell to his knees and began to topple over, Gabriel put his hands together and swung from the heels, catching him in the side of the head. The big kid was down and out in two blows, and Gabe jumped on him. He might have really injured him if some adults hadn't come running to break it up.

All that day in school I worried about what might happen in the alley later. I knew what Ryan had gone through. I didn't want to fight. I knew it was wrong. I really wanted to do what I had advised Ryan to do: to talk to Gabriel, to tell him there was no reason to fight, that we could be friends.

I tried to pray about it, but it was as if my prayers weren't going anywhere. I felt as if God wasn't listening, and I wondered why. Maybe it was because He knew that I knew that there had to be a better way than people slugging it out with each other.

The more I thought about it, the more scared I was. All of a sudden, I couldn't concentrate on one thing my teacher said. When I tried to read, my mind wandered. Finally, I knew exactly how Ryan felt the first time he was threatened. He had run to his bike and was home so fast that no one had a chance to catch him, even though Gabriel hadn't even been aware of the problem yet.

Today was the day. Gabriel had been told, and Ryan and I were to be the victims. One thing I was sure of: no way Ryan was going to show up in that alley. I'd have bet my life on that. News of the fight spread quickly throughout the school, and when we broke for morning recess, everyone in my class wanted to hear about it.

"I don't know any more about it than what Mike said this morning," I said. "He's probably lying. I haven't been invited to any fight. Anyway, I have no problem with Gabriel Irving. Neither does Ryan. No way Ryan's walking into that, and I'd be crazy to."

"You're not going?" Jimmy asked. "You want a reputation as a coward?"

"I don't care that much about my reputation," I said, trying to convince myself. "I'd rather be known as somebody who doesn't resort to fighting about everything."

Jimmy shook his head. "I just hope you don't look bad in this, Dal."

"What do I care? If I fight, I get a reputation like Mike Ancona and Gabe Irving. Who wants that?"

"Who wants to be thought of as a coward?"

"Jimmy, there's a difference between being a coward and being wise enough to stay above that sort of thing. Anyway, remember we have basketball practice at my place right after school so Ryan won't have to be out alone after dark."

Jimmy just walked away, shaking his head.

At lunchtime our class played Mike Ancona's in basketball as usual. Ryan didn't even show up to watch. Jimmy played well, but Mike was fantastic. I found myself playing very carefully, not showing up Mike, trying to be nice to him. If I had been doing it because I was a Christian, to try to win him over, I would have been happy. But I was miserable. The real reason I was doing it, I knew, was to try to get Mike to call the whole thing off.

I wanted him to see that I was a nice guy, as if he didn't know that already. My tune had really changed from before school. Rather than acting like the big, brave, tough guy, I was cautious and careful. I was hoping he could just forget about everything and tell Gabe Irving not to waste his time with us.

His team beat ours badly, and my teammates kept looking at me as if it was my fault. I had made only two baskets, and Mike, the man I was supposed to be guarding, scored more than half their points. I hate to admit it, but I didn't care. I would have done anything to not antagonize him any more.

That afternoon, about an hour before the end of school, I had a plan. "Jim," I said, "let's get out of here quick after school. I want to get home and get changed and have everything ready for practice."

"Are you kidding?" he said. "You may not be going to the alley, but I am. I want to see what happens."

"I'm not going to be there, and you know Ryan won't either."

"I'll bet you'll both be there. Ryan is counting on your sticking up for him."

"Ryan's a chicken. You saw that yesterday."

"Yeah, and today you're the chicken."

"I *do* want to get ready for practice."

"I'm sure you do, but how long does that take?"

"Long enough."

He shook his head. "I never thought I'd see the day, Dallas."

"What?"

"I never thought I'd see you acting like a coward."

"I'm *not!*"

"What do you call it?"

"Wisdom."

Jimmy waved me off with a sneer. "Admit it, O'Neil. You're yellow."

I knew he was right, and I felt like a liar to not be able to admit it. "How would *you* feel?" I asked him.

"I'd be chicken of Gabriel Irving, but *I'd* admit it."

"You're not going to go home with me after school then?"

"I'll be there in time for practice."

"Are you going to say anything about my not showing up?"

"No, Dallas. Your secret is safe with me."

The way he said that made me feel like a fool. That doubled the way I was feeling, but it didn't change my mind.

51

When the bell rang, I raced for my bike. As I rode away, I heard friends calling out messages of encouragement. "Kill him, Dallas!" they said. "We know you can. See you in the alley!"

I had to go by the alley on the way home, and I didn't want anyone to know I wasn't showing up for the fight. Since the junior high wouldn't be letting out for several more minutes, I rode straight to the alley. If people thought I looked brave and eager to get on with it, that was OK. I knew that by the next day, everyone would know I had chickened out.

Oh, I could say that I didn't know anything about it, but everyone would know the truth. If I really didn't know anything about it, I would have been the only kid in the school who didn't.

I rode to and through the alley. No one was there yet. I sped on home, not looking to the right or the left or behind me.

My mother greeted me warmly, and I helped her carry groceries in from the car. Then I swept the driveway and changed the net on our rim, feeling the whole time that I wasn't where I was supposed to be. Yet I was relieved, too, to not be where I didn't want to be.

Jack Bastable was the first player to show up. His special school for retarded kids gets out earlier than our school and the schools of the others. I enjoyed having someone to talk to who didn't know anything about Mike Ancona or Gabriel Irving. A few of the others arrived from their schools and started shooting around.

About half an hour later, Jimmy arrived with a couple more from our school. They glared at me, but when I looked at them, they looked away.

"How you guys doin'?" I asked.

"We're doing fine," Jimmy said. "Which is more than we can say for Ryan."

"What do you mean?"

"I s'pose you'd like to know what happened."

"Sure I would," I said, as the others gathered around. "What happened?"

"Well, unlike someone else we know who should have been there, Ryan showed up. He probably wishes he hadn't. At the very least, Dallas, he wishes you had."

7

Mud

Jimmy told the story.

"I got there with a bunch of other guys, and Ryan was already there, just straddling his bike, waiting to see what was going to happen. I'd say about a hundred kids were there. Ryan looked scared to death. He also kept looking around for you, Dallas."

I felt bad enough without Jimmy's rubbing it in.

"Mike Ancona comes running with Gabriel Irving and asks Ryan, 'Where's yer chicken friend?'

" 'I don't know,' Ryan says. 'Maybe he doesn't wanna fight any more'n I do.'

"Ancona laughs and looks at Irving, but Irving isn't laughing. He says, 'Ancona, you bring me over here to fight this little kid? Where's the hotshot athlete you were tellin' me about?' Ancona says it looks like he chickened out, so Irving whispers to him for a minute and starts walkin' away. 'Let me know when you've got a real job for me,' he says, and he leaves."

"He left?" I asked.

"Yup. Took off. Now Ancona looks embarrassed, and a little worried. Ryan's got a lot of friends there. So he says, ''OK, how 'bout just you and me, and you tell your friends to stay out of it?'

"Ryan says, 'I don't want anybody else involved in it, but I don't want to be involved in it either. Let's just be friends.' Well, at first it looks like Mike's gonna take him up on it.

"He says, 'You know, Ryan. I think you're right. I've already had my shot at you, and I wouldn't mind gettin' my hands on O'Neil. But I'm gonna let Gabe handle him. You and me, we can just shake and call a truce. How's that sound?'

"Well, Ryan says that sounds great to him, and as Mike comes over to him, Ryan starts getting off his bike. Right while he's got one leg comin' over the top, Mike jumps up and kicks the bike and Ryan goes down underneath it. As he's struggling to get out from under it, Mike jumps on it, pressing all that metal into Ryan's legs, and he's screamin' like everything.

"Mike says, 'You agreed your friends would stay out of this, didn't you?' Ryan was crying already, but he nodded, and Mike popped him a couple, right in the face. Gave him a fat lip and a black eye, and while Ryan was lying there, not able to get out from under his own bike, Mike jumps on it again, breaking a few spokes in each wheel. Then he took off, calling over his shoulder, 'Now you and I are even. Just tell O'Neil he's next!' "

"That trick must have been what Irving whispered to him," I said. "That's his style, to sucker punch somebody."

"Well, that's great, Dallas," Jimmy said. "You're a big help now."

"I had no idea Ryan would be there," I said. "How could I know that?"

Jimmy shrugged. "Maybe you should have known he was braver than you."

"That's not fair!" I said.

"Maybe you're right," he said. "But don't you think we could skip practice and go see how Ryan's doing?"

We mounted our bikes and rode to his house. Ryan's mother was surprised to see us but assured us he was well enough to have visitors. He was stretched out on the living room couch.

"Actually, I feel pretty good," he said.

"Why?"

"Because I know Dallas is going to keep his promise. Aren't you, Dal?"

"What promise?"

"You said if I got hurt, no matter who did it, you were comin' after Mike. Isn't that what you said?"

"Yeah, but don't you think there's been enough fighting?"

He glared at me. "You must have thought so. Where were you today when I needed you?"

"I was there this morning when I didn't even know you needed help," I said.

"That was great," he said, "but that's also when you made your promise. I thought sure if I got beat up, it would be by Gabriel Irving. But this is even better, Dallas. You can take Mike for me again, and you don't even have to fight Gabriel."

"What makes you think Mike won't sic Gabriel on me?"

"What if he does? I saw him! He's no bigger than Mike. I know you can take him."

"Don't be too sure."

"Anyway, you said you would go after Mike if I got hurt, and I got hurt." He sure had. He looked terrible. His face was puffy and bruised and swollen, and his lip was split. "My mom was gonna call the school and get Mike in trouble," he said. "But I talked her out of it. That wouldn't end anything. Anyway, I don't want to be thought of as a coward who gets his mommy after everybody."

I looked at the floor. I knew I was going to be considered the coward I was, and I didn't know what to do about it. I knew I would have to have it out with Mike. There was no way around it. And that would mean facing Gabriel sometime. Now that was something to dread. But I'd have to face that when it came up.

"One thing I know for sure right now," I said, smiling. "When we play the Condors, I'm putting Big Jack on Mike Ancona."

I thought that was pretty funny, but no one laughed.

"You'd better handle Mike yourself and soon," Jimmy said, "or your name will be mud."

My name was mud the next day anyway. People I didn't even know called me a coward, and I got dirty looks from most of my friends. Lucky for me, Jimmy was finally on my side. He said he still didn't understand why I hadn't showed up in the alley the day before, but he wasn't going to quit being my friend over it.

At lunchtime, before our basketball game, I asked Mike if I could talk to him.

"Depends, chicken," he said in front of the others. "What about?"

"About yesterday."

"Yeah, where were you, hot stuff?"

"That doesn't matter. I'm here now, and you're gonna come and have a talk with me."

"And if I don't?"

"Just like yesterday morning, you're going to wish you had."

"We could talk in the alley," he taunted, "but you probably wouldn't show up."

A few people snickered.

"You wouldn't have shown up alone yesterday," I said. "You're nothing without your friend."

"Same as Ryan," he said. "He's nothin' without you."

"Yeah, but you beat up on him anyway. So now you have to take yours, without your protection around. I told you I would come after you if he got hurt, and he got hurt."

"Yeah, but now we're even, and we have a truce. You can't break that."

"I can't break *your* truce?! I have to do what I said I was going to do. Come with me."

"And if I don't?"

"Then I'll drop you right where you stand."

I saw fear in his eyes for the first time. He followed me, but so did a lot of other kids. I turned on them. "This is private, so buzz off." They watched from a distance.

"What're you gonna do?" he asked.

"You're lucky," I said, as we stood near where he had tried to beat up Ryan the morning before. "I don't believe in fighting, except in self-defense. And I don't believe in picking on guys who are smaller than me. But still, you beat up Ryan, and so you have to pay."

"How?"

"I want you to get behind those trees over there and not come out until two o'clock."

"I'll be late for school!"

"I know. And when you're asked why you're late, you say nothing about me. I'll be able to see you if you come back early, because our classroom windows are in sight of those trees."

"So what if I don't do what you say?"

"Then I'll have to do to you what you did to Ryan."

"This doesn't make any sense, O'Neil."

"You haven't been making sense since Ryan made you look bad on the basketball court the other day."

"So, that's it? I just stay hiding in the trees until two o'clock?"

"Better than getting beat up, isn't it?"

"I guess. And then we're even, and we can call a truce?"

"That's up to you. You still siccing Gabriel Irving on me?"

"That's for me to know and you to find out."

As I left him he was moving behind the trees. I knew I couldn't really follow through on keeping him out of school. It wasn't right, and if it got back to my parents I'd never be able to explain it. Grown-ups think that kids should take care of fights by reporting the fighters, but kids know that that usually makes it worse.

When I got to the school building, I told the coach that Mike Ancona was out in the trees. "So, if he's late getting back in from lunch, you know where he is."

"What's he doing out there?" the coach said.

"Ask him," I said.

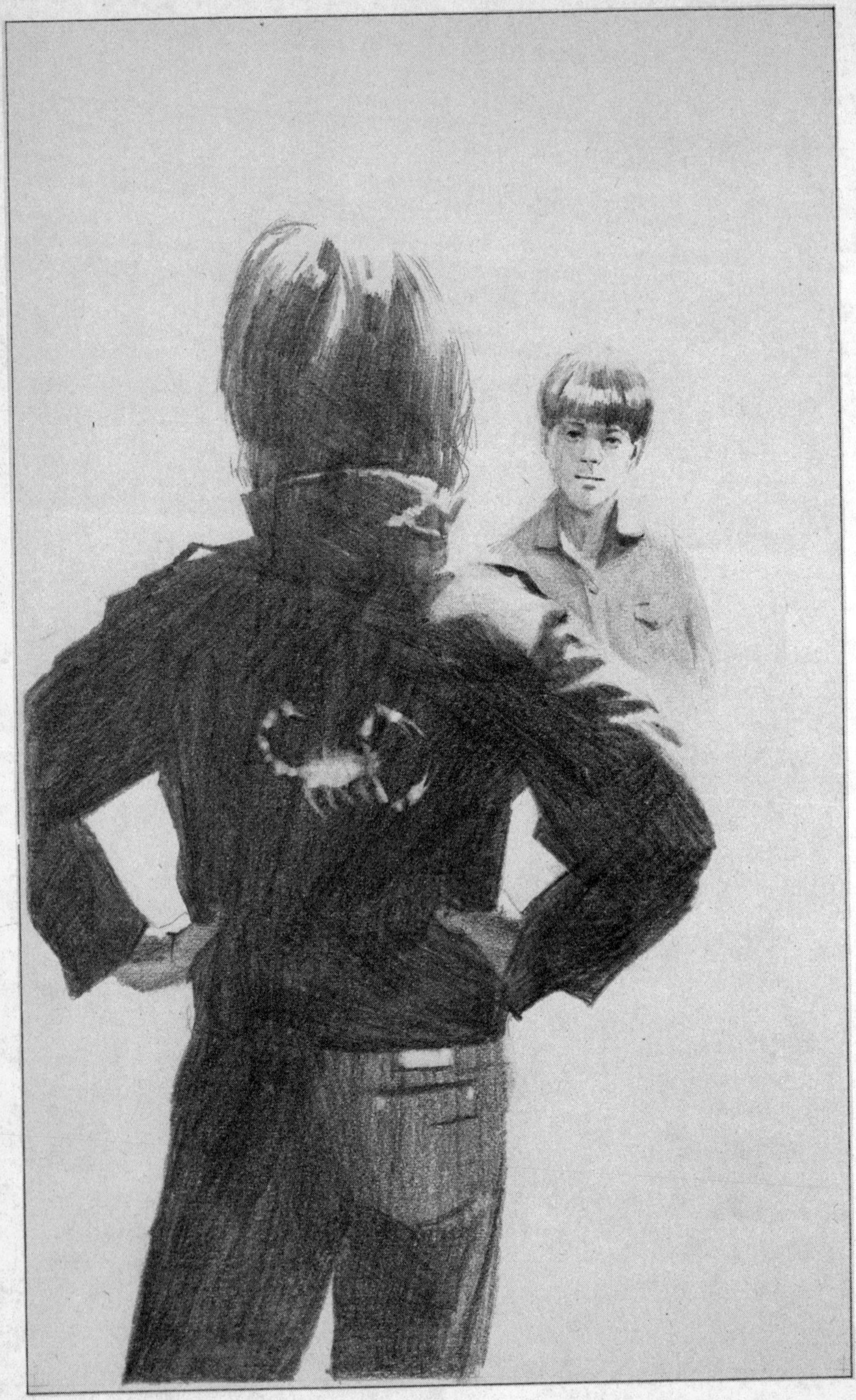

8

No Way Out

I wasn't in class a minute before I saw the coach trudging across the playground toward the trees. When he came back with Mike, the coach was gesturing and scolding. Mike wasn't saying anything. I felt good. Mike was in trouble, but he hadn't really missed any school. Best of all, he couldn't tell the coach why he had hidden in the trees. That would have really made him look wimpy.

I was frustrated anyway. What was I supposed to do now? People were going to be asking why I hadn't at least smashed Mike in the face for what he did to Ryan. What kind of a friend and protector was I? Was it good enough to say I was doing what I thought Jesus would do?

The problem was that I was really acting more out of fear than because of Christ's example. I knew He was usually non-violent and that when one of His disciples cut off a soldier's ear, Jesus healed it and told His friends not to fight for Him. But there was also the time that He saw men making His Father's house into a place for buying and selling. He was violent then. Maybe He didn't actually hurt anybody, but maybe He did. He used a whip, and He turned over tables and bird cages. That means there *is* a time for action, but how was I supposed to know when that was and what exactly I should do?

When our class went outside for afternoon recess, Mike's class was coming in.

I pulled him off to the side. "Listen," I said, "I need to talk with you."

"Hey!" he said. "It wasn't my fault that Coach found me. I did what you said. We're even."

"Who do you think told the coach?" I said.

He shrugged. "You're crazy, O'Neil."

"Just do me a favor, all right?"

"What?"

"Get Gabriel Irving to meet with me, just the two of us, one-on-one."

"What for?"

"I just want to talk with him, that's all."

"Sure. You're probably gonna sucker punch him."

"No, that's *his* game, not mine. I'm serious. I just want to talk to him. The whole point is to avoid a fight."

Mike looked disbelieving. "Right."

"You'll do it?"

"I'll tell him what you said, but don't count on it."

"Why not?"

"Because I also already told him what you said about him yesterday. That he was a sissy and afraid to face you alone."

"Well, I guess I'll have to stand by that statement then. Either he meets with me alone, or he's really a coward."

"Nobody's as much a coward as you were yesterday, O'Neil."

I couldn't argue with that. But that was yesterday. I wasn't any less scared today. But I would meet with Gabriel. And if he attacked me, I'd have to fight. Otherwise, I wouldn't.

I had to have been dreaming to think that Mike would give Gabriel the straight message and that Gabriel would agree to it. Maybe Mike told him what I wanted; I don't know. All I know is that when I left school that day, Mike ran up to me and told me where to wait for Gabriel. It wasn't in the alley. It was on a side street between the schools.

A crowd had started to gather, and Jimmy rode up too. I asked him to watch my bike, then asked the others to leave. "There's not going to be any fight. We're just talking. In fact, with people around, we're not even going to talk."

Some of the kids left. Most didn't.

I didn't have to wait long. Mike and Gabriel came from the direction of the junior high with a crowd of their own following not far behind. If someone hadn't known better, he might have thought this was going to be a major rumble, a gang fight between the schools. More of the kids from our crowd took off when they saw the bigger kids coming.

"I want to talk to you alone, Gabe," I called out, trying to sound calm. I knew I was failing. "I don't even want Mike in on it."

"Fair enough," Gabriel said with a sneer. "But he doesn't have to stay far away, and neither do my other friends."

"No deal," I said. "I want to talk to you alone."

"Who do you think you are?" he demanded, stopping about twenty feet away from me. "You think you can make deals with me? Forget it!"

"All I want to do is talk to you alone, Gabriel. Now if you don't want to do that, I guess *you're* the coward."

"You don't want to be calling me a coward, O'Neil. You're the one who didn't show up yesterday, and it cost your little friend, didn't it?"

"Yeah, and I suppose that sucker punch of Mike's was your idea!"

Gabriel only laughed. "We're wasting time," he said. "You think you can take me or not?"

"One-on-one you don't stand a chance," I said, not as sure as I sounded.

"Ha! Try me, man!"

"Not with all your friends around."

"I'll tell them to stay out of it. You do the same."

"My friends aren't here," I said. "I'm keeping my end of the bargain."

Gabriel turned and looked at his friends, then at the crowd behind me. "All right," he said, speaking more softly and heading toward me slowly. "Let's talk."

I watched him carefully as I moved his way. One false move and I was going to pop him one. I didn't want to. I didn't even want to fight. But I was not going to be sucker punched.

When he got within five feet of me he asked a strange question. "You want my guys to turn their backs on us?"

I shrugged. "That's not necessary. I want to talk to you because I don't want to fight with you."

"Yeah, but see, I *want* to fight with *you*."

"Why, Gabriel? This hassle was between Mike and me, and it's all over now."

"No! No it wasn't! Mike told me the hassle was between that little kid and him."

"Ryan."

"Yeah, Ryan. So why were *you* involved?"

"Because Mike's bigger than Ryan and was going to hurt him. In fact, yesterday he *did* hurt him."

"And you got involved again, so now it's my turn. You're bigger than Mike, so that's why you beat him up today."

"I've never beat up *anybody!*"

"You beat up Mike today."

"I did not!"

"You're a liar. He told me you took him out in the trees and beat him up, but you were careful not to leave any marks on his face."

"That's not true! If he told you the truth you'd know I didn't lay a hand on him. All I did was make him wait in the trees, and then I sent the coach out to bring him in."

Gabriel grunted. "What a story! You defended *your* little friend, and now I'm gonna defend *my* little friend."

"I don't want to fight you, Gabriel."

"Of course you don't. Nobody does. You want my guys to turn their backs?"

"No, I want to talk."

"What do you want to say?"

"I want a truce."

"If I were you, I'd want a truce too. You're a chicken, O'Neil. Face it."

"How would you feel if you found out I was telling the truth about Mike today?"

"It would just make you seem like more of a wimp."

"Wimp or not, it's the truth."

Gabriel motioned for me to lean close, as if he was going to tell me a secret, and like an idiot, I almost fell for it.

I was just stepping toward him when I noticed he was setting his feet for leverage so he could get in the first punch. I hesitated and stepped back. "What about your guys?" I asked, trying to distract him.

"You want them to turn their backs?"

I didn't know how many times he'd asked me that question, so I figured there must be something to it. "Yeah, all right," I said. "I want them to turn their backs."

He raised his fist without turning around, and over his shoulder I saw at least fifteen guys in black leather jackets turn around. On their backs was emblazoned a large splotch of red material.

"What's that?" I asked.

"Would you recognize it if you saw it up close?" he asked.

"I don't know. Would I?"

He turned and showed his back to me.

I leaned forward, squinting. "Is that a scorpion?"

Without turning around, he answered. "We're the Red Scorpions, and these jackets cost over a hundred dollars each."

"Where do you get the money?"

He turned around slowly. "I could have karate kicked you while you were lookin' at my scorpion, jerk," he said. "And I could take you out right now if I wanted to."

"No, you couldn't have, and no, you can't," I said, not so sure. "I know you're a cheating sucker puncher, and I was ready for that."

"But if you don't want me to beat you up right here and right now with my guys all around, you can pay me, oh, say, five dollars a week until the end of the school year."

"You want me to pay protection money?"

"We've got to pay for our jackets and fun, man."

"Maybe *you* do, but *I* don't."

"Yes, you do. If you don't want to suffer."

"To me it would be worse to pay a creep like you."

"OK, you want me to call in the guys to work you over?"

"No, I want to see if you can do it yourself."

"Let me think about it a minute," he said, resting his chin in his hand and cocking his head. "All right, listen, here's what we'll do." He motioned me close, but I was ready.

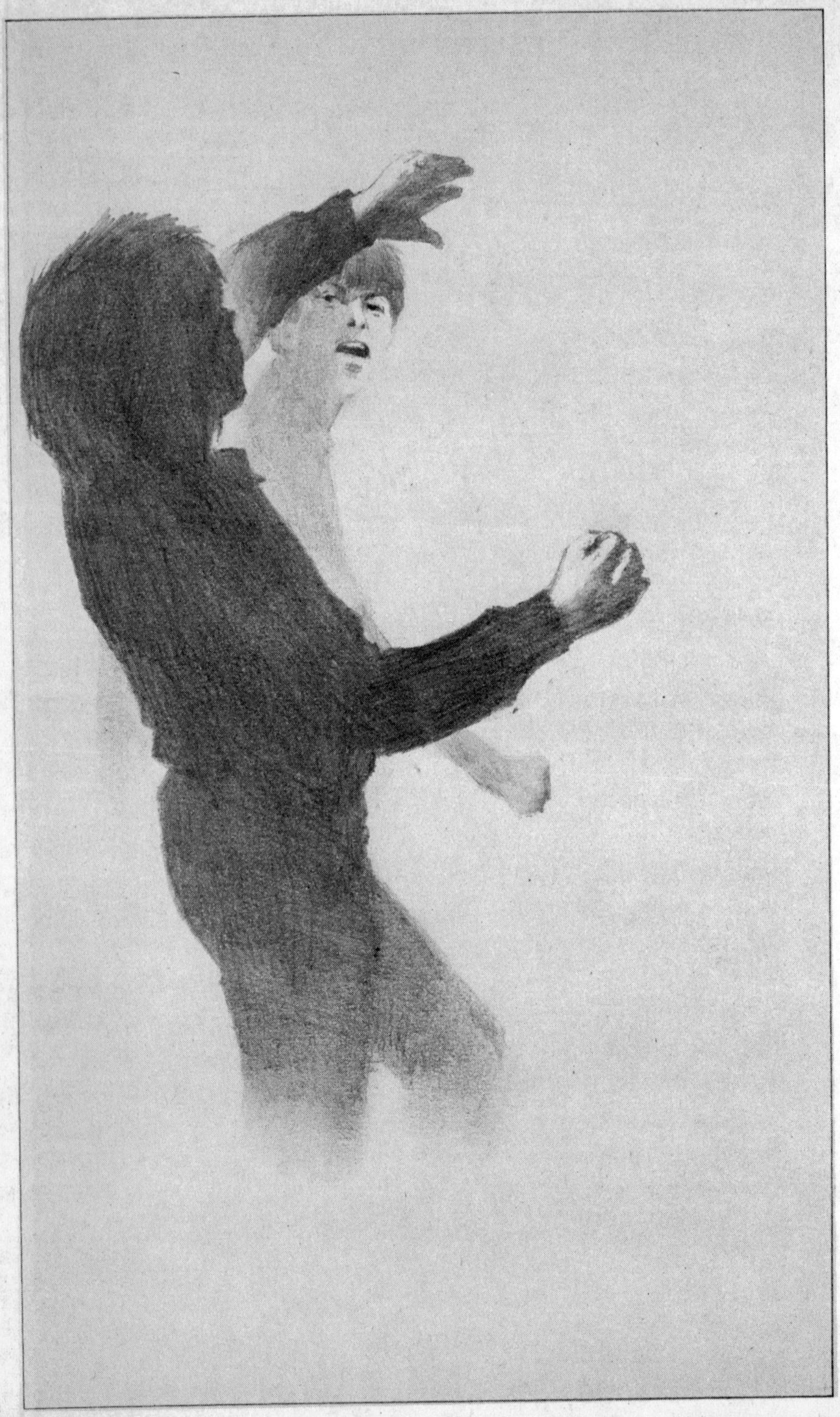

9

The Fight

I don't know where I got the courage, but when Gabriel Irving leaned in as if to whisper to me and I saw him clench his fists, I slid back on my heels and shot out a left jab to his chin that caught him flush. He rocked back, his eyes wild. He tried to keep his balance, but he sat down. A bluish mark immediately arose on his chin, and he rubbed it hard.

He tried to smile, but tears welled in his eyes. I couldn't believe my luck. I had stunned him, hurt him, and now he was wild with anger. As soon as he was back on his feet, he lunged at me, swinging wildly. I side-stepped his flailing arms and shot out the same left jab. Miraculously, it caught him in the exact spot it had before. Even I winced as he fell in a heap, gingerly protecting his chin.

I knew he was finished. I could tell he wanted to quit. But he was a tough guy. He had a reputation to worry about. He had to get back up and keep coming. Plus, he had help. I knew it wouldn't be long before he asked for their help.

He charged me again, kicking this time. The first kick caught me in the knee but didn't hurt much. I took a page out of his book and dropped to my other knee, pretending he had hurt me. When he surged in to kick again, I grabbed his foot, stood up, and twisted. I made him hop on the other foot and drove him back, not letting go of his foot.

He slid on his back, tearing his leather jacket and—I was sure—ripping the scorpion half off. Now he was as mad as I'd ever seen him, but I didn't have time to look up to see if his fellow gang members were coming to help him or if I had anywhere to run. I thought I had proved that I wasn't a coward, and no one would have thought I was crazy to get out of there and not face those odds. But here he came again.

This time he didn't quit charging until he had me in a bear hug and tried to throw me to the ground. I felt myself losing balance and skipping in short steps to stay upright, and suddenly there was a sharp pain in my neck and I felt warm liquid running into my shirt. He had bitten me! He had sunk his teeth into my neck and drawn blood!

I planted my right foot and slung him till he almost flew off me, and while his head was whizzing past, I shot out a roundhouse left and caught him flush on the cheek. I don't think I broke anything, but I could sure feel all the bones on that side of his face.

His eyes were within two inches of mine, and I could see my blood on his mouth. His eyes were dazed, and he began to crumple. I was ready to follow with a right hand, but I didn't want to kill him. I thought he would be down and out, but his eyes cleared even before he hit the ground.

He tried to bear hug me again, so I clubbed his right cheek from the other side. That spun him around. I could hear kids yelling and screaming, and I was certain the rest of the Red Scorpions were coming. I sneaked a peek past Gabriel and saw them just standing there, looking as surprised as he was.

I knew they weren't afraid of me, not that many kids. Maybe they thought that all the kids who had come from my school were on my side and would fight if they had to. That wasn't true. I decided that if I had to hit Gabriel one more time, I was going to need an escape route. Jimmy stood straddling his bike and holding mine.

Gabriel came charging in one more time. This time he wasn't flailing. He was just coming at me, reaching with both arms as if trying to tackle me or hug me or something. I took careful aim and popped him one on the chin again. He screamed in pain but didn't hold his chin. He grabbed my shirt and wouldn't let go. I started to spin free, but he was still there. And here came the Scorpions.

I turned to run toward my bike, but Gabriel was a dead weight, holding me back. I decided I would have to turn and sock him one more time to get free, and now I was frantic.

I stopped and whirled and cocked my fist, but he drew even closer, his face next to my head. "Don't hit me again," he squealed. "Help me! Save me!"

Save *him?!* What was *that* all about?

"Go!" he shouted. "Go! Go!" But he was still holding on. I couldn't shake him. I turned and ran toward my bike. Jimmy let go of it, and Gabriel jumped on with me. "Go!" he screamed again. "Go!"

The Scorpions, on foot, were in hot pursuit. I was more than confused. I was totally in the dark. I pedaled as hard as I could, trying to get up some speed in spite of all the extra weight. Jimmy was pulling away, headed toward Baker Street.

"Where do you want to go, Gabe?"

"Your place! Anyplace! Just go!"

I was able to go just faster than the pursuing Red Scorpions, who ran through the crowd from my school as if they weren't there. It's a good thing I hadn't expected anybody to defend me. They turned and ran. The Scorpions ignored them and kept chasing us, shouting threats.

But the threats weren't aimed at me. They were aimed at Gabriel. "What's this all about, Irving?" I demanded.

"Just keep pedaling, O'Neil!"

I did, until I was so tired I could hardly move. About a mile from my house, when we were already in the country, I pulled off the road and stopped. "You wanna pedal for a while?" I asked, gasping.

"Sure, but hurry up."

I couldn't imagine why he wanted me to hurry now. Surely we had outrun all his friends—or were they enemies?—by now. I got off and switched places with him, and he started hopping and running and pedaling all at the same time. I tried to get situated on the bike, which kept him off balance, and he took as long as I had to get going. I looked behind us and was shocked to see three Red Scorpions still chasing us on foot.

"Are those guys long distance runners?" I asked.

"No, but they're in good shape. If we don't keep moving, they'll catch us."

"They look out of breath to me," I said.

"*I'm* out of breath, and I've been *riding!*" Gabe said. "A few hundred more yards and we'll lose them."

"I hope so. I don't want them to know where I live."

"You think they don't know where *you* live? I'll prove they do. I'll ride right to it."

And he did.

When we got into my dusty driveway, I could see my mother and my two little sisters bent over in the garden forty acres away. I waved. My mother waved and pointed to the house. I knew what she meant. My snack was in the refrigerator. I knew what my chores were. And homework had to be done before dinner.

"C'mon in," I told Gabriel. Jimmy would meet me later at practice.

I don't know if Gabe felt as out of place as he looked, but he sure looked awkward. I opened the door and waited until he was finished looking all around our place, then I followed him inside. His jacket was a mess, and the red scorpion had been almost ripped off the back.

"Let me take your coat," I said. "You can sit over there."

He slipped off his jacket, and I set it on the back of a chair. I got my plate of cookies and glass of milk from the refrigerator and set them before him. He looked at me wide-eyed as I got more cookies and milk for myself and sat across the table from him.

"Go ahead," I said. I nibbled at a cookie while Gabriel devoured his whole stack.

"Hungry," he said.

"Obviously," I said, smiling. "You want something for that chin?"

"Like what?"

"An ice pack?"

"Nah."

"Doesn't that sound good?" I knew it did, but he didn't want to admit it. I slid the rest of my cookies over to him, and as he started in on them, I got two washcloths, dampened them, and wrapped each around three ice cubes. I put one on my neck and gave the other to him. "Just hold it up to your chin. Careful. It'll hurt at first."

He hissed in pain as he gingerly touched the pack to his face. He jerked it away, then slowly nestled his chin into it. His eyes were shut tight, and as he relaxed I wondered if he was asleep. I was more curious than I'd ever been about anything, but I didn't want to ask him about his friends-turned-enemies until I thought he was ready.

"Why don't you just sit here and rest while I do my chores," I suggested.

"Chores? You do chores?"

"Sure, don't you?"

"No way. I guess my mom figures I have to come home to an empty apartment every day for three hours, so cooking dinner for her and me is all she expects."

"You cook dinner? I've never done that."

"So, what are your chores?"

"Well, today I have to carry a fifty-pound salt block down to the water softener in the basement. And then I have to bring the clean laundry up and divide it between all the dressers."

"All the dressers?"

"Yeah. My sisters' and my parents' and mine."

He nodded slowly. "Can I watch?"

"It's not very exciting."

"Yeah, but I still want to watch."

"OK, on one condition. You have to tell me what happened out there today."

He nodded and followed me out to the back porch where my dad stored the salt blocks. I snagged one with a rusty pair of old-fashioned ice tongs, bent my knees, and let it hang between my legs as I shuffled through the house and down the stairs. Gabriel followed me. His face was red and puffy except for the black and blue mark on his chin.

"That heavy?" he asked.

"What do you think?"

"Where do you put it?"

"Right here in this cylinder."

"Let me try it?"

"If you want to."

I set it on the floor, and he grabbed the ice tongs. He couldn't get the block more than a couple of inches off the ground. "No wonder you kicked the stuffing out me today," he said.

I lowered the block into the softener and moved to the baskets of folded and stacked clothes near the dryer.

"Want me to carry one of those?" Gabe asked.

"No, thanks. Watch this." I put one basket atop the other, held the bottom one and tucked the edge of the top one under my chin. I started up the stairs and didn't stop until I was all the way up to my sisters' third-floor bedroom.

Within five minutes I had all the clothes put away in everyone's rooms. "Now, if I didn't have a guest, I would do my homework before dinner and have everything out of the way so I could practice basketball with the guys for a couple of hours."

Gabriel sat on my bed shaking his head. "What a life," he said.

"Good or bad?" I asked.

"Boring."

"Not to me. I don't like doing chores so much, but I like helping out, and I really like having everything done so I can do what I want."

"Why are you being so nice to me, O'Neil?"

"I'll tell you, Gabriel, but first you can quit calling me by my last name. You don't have to impress me now. There's nobody around. We're not in the street, and we're not fighting. Anyway, you owe me some answers first."

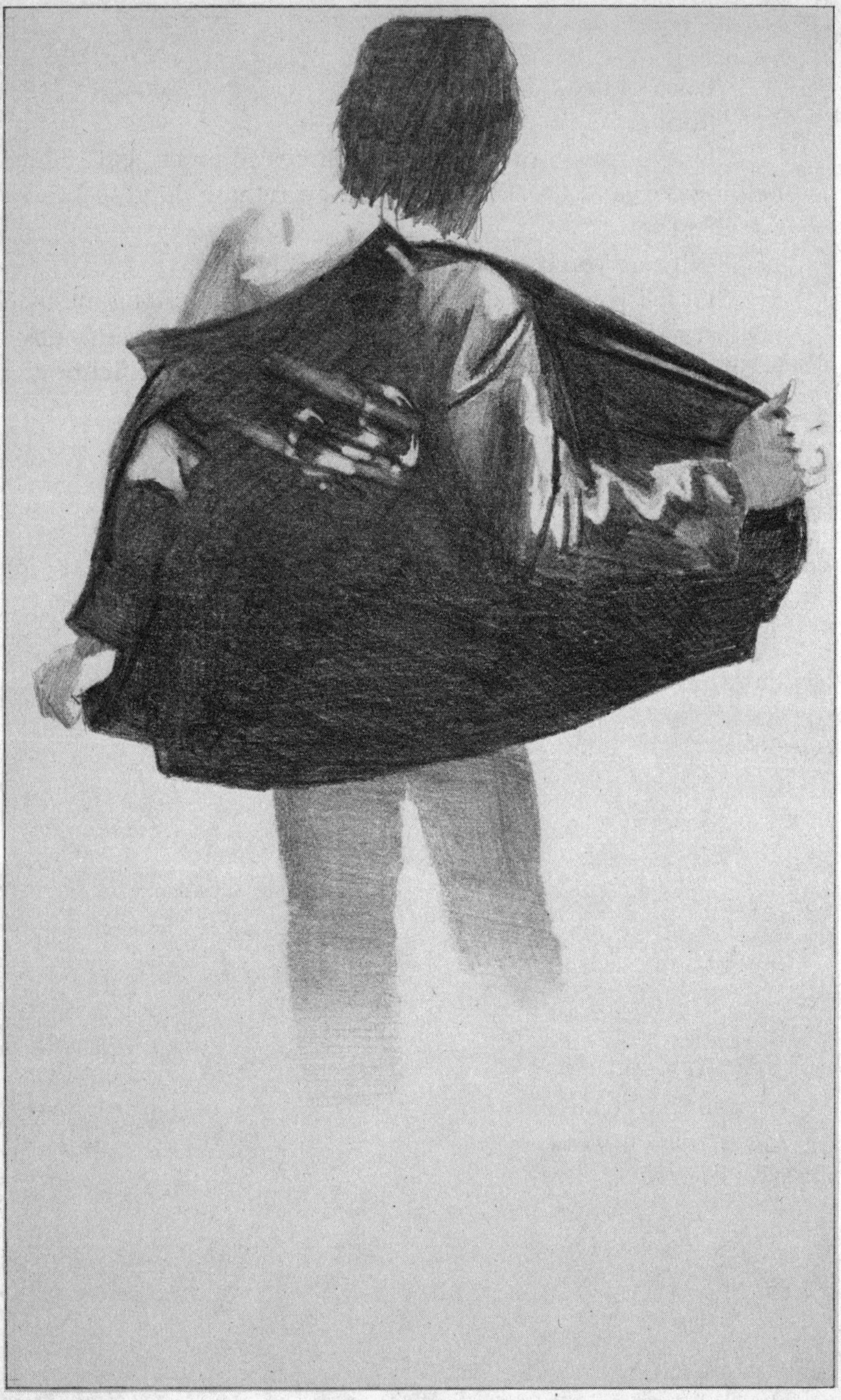

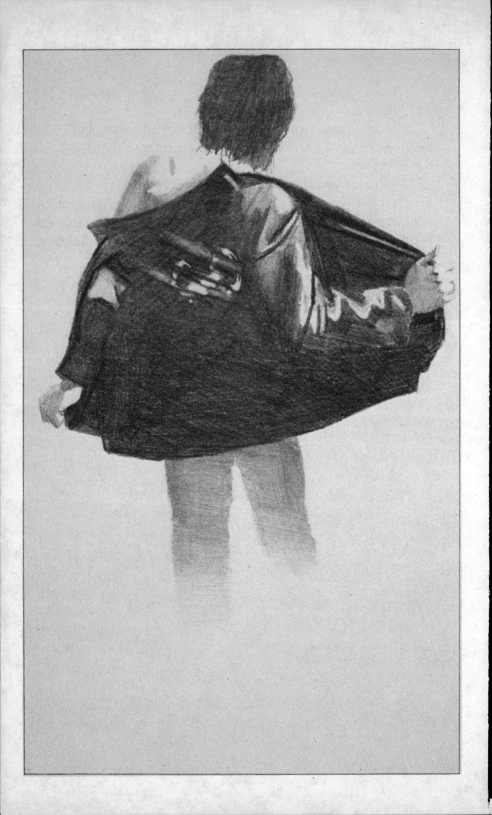

10

The Shock

I motioned for Gabriel to follow me back down to the kitchen. We sat where we sat before. "What in the world happened today?" I asked.

"What do you think?" he said.

"Well, I thought you were part of a gang. Aren't you?"

"I was the leader."

"But you're not now?"

"I'm as good as dead now."

"I don't understand."

"Man, O'Neil, you live so far out in the sticks that you don't know anything."

"I know your gang didn't help you out when you needed it."

"Well, it's a strange gang. We have our own rules. I've been in charge for a year and a half. Anybody in the gang, me included, can fight anyone he wants and have help from the rest, but only in finishing him off."

"Finishing him off?"

"Well, not killing anybody, of course, but if I had beat you up today, you'd have looked a lot worse than I do right now. You probably would have been in the hospital."

"So, why didn't they help you?"

"That's not how we do it. Any Red Scorpion who gets beat loses his standing in the gang. Today I was the biggest loser in a long time. Everybody moves up a notch. My lieutenants have been gunning for me for months. Once I get beat up, they can finish me off. You hurt me, but you were good to me compared to what they would have done if they'd caught me."

"Why? It doesn't make sense!"

"It makes sense to us. To get to the top of the gang, I had to challenge anybody above me. Four guys regretted letting me challenge them. Four others just let me move up past them. When they saw me go down today, a lot of people wanted a piece of me."

"What about when they see you tomorrow?"

"They won't. I'm gonna lay low, play sick, skip school. By the time I get back, my bruises will look real bad, and I'll just let everybody who wants to pass me up. Except the little guys or the wimps, of course."

"Where will that put you in the gang?"

"Bottom fourth somewhere."

"You'll still want to be in it?"

"It's my life, man. Isn't your whole life wrapped up in your gang?"

"I'm not in a gang."

Gabriel Irving squinted at me. "You think I don't know that the Baker Street Sports Club is a front for a gang and that almost everybody in it is as tough as you?"

I laughed. "Ryan and I are the only ones who have fought anybody in the last year, and none of us have ever fought each other, except for maybe a little skirmish in the middle of a game."

He just sat there shaking his head. "What a life," he said.

"How do you like *your* life, Gabe?"

"It's all right."

"You said the Scorpions were your life, but now they're all out to get you."

For once he was silent. I asked him if he'd like to join me at basketball practice after dinner and whether he had to call his mother.

"She's workin' tonight anyway," he said. " 'S long as I'm home by eleven, I'm cool."

"You'll be home by nine," I promised. "My dad will drive you."

I got permission for him to eat with us, and my dad agreed to drive him home when we got back from basketball. Gabriel acted like a tough guy through dinner, and my sisters were both scared of him and intrigued by him. When they asked about his injuries, my parents interrupted and changed the subject. I knew I would have some explaining to do to them later.

The guys were stunned to see Gabriel Irving at practice, especially Ryan who almost ran off.

I told them, "Make our guest feel welcome."

They all greeted him. Several encouraged him to take a few shots. He kept saying he wasn't any good, and when they talked him into shooting anyway, he proved it. He was embarrassed, then pretended there was something wrong with the court or the ball or the rim or his shoes or something and sat down to watch us.

He pretended to be bored, but he didn't miss a thing. On the way to his apartment he asked a lot of questions. "Are all the guys in your club religious?"

I tried to explain that those of us who were Christians believed in a Person, not in a church or a religion. I told him that not everybody in the Baker Street Sports Club was a Christian, but that those who weren't at least knew what we were all about and respected us. "We're working on them," I added with a smile.

"I s'pose next you're gonna want to work on me."

"I already worked on you a little today, didn't I?" I said. It was the first time I had seen him smile. I felt sorry for him.

"You sure did," he said.

81

"No hard feelings?"

"Are you kidding? You saved my life."

"I felt a little guilty getting off the first punch when I really don't even believe in fighting."

He looked at me and cocked his head. "Guilty? If you hadn't sucker punched me I would have sucker punched you, and the whole fight would have turned out different. My whole life would have turned out different."

"Your whole life?"

"I told you the Scorpions were my life, man. You think I'll ever be the leader again?"

"Do you want to be?"

"Course."

"Really?"

"Course!"

"Sorry to say this, Gabe, but what kind of a life is that, always worrying that your own gang members are out to get you? If I worried about that in the Baker Street Sports Club, I'd quit right now."

"Those guys aren't jealous of you? They don't want your job?"

"Not that I know of."

He shook his head. "Maybe I should join *your* club."

"You'd be our first member from outside this area, and we have lots of rules."

"I was just kiddin', Dallas. I wouldn't really wanna be associated with a bunch of goody-two-shoes athletes like you."

But I could tell he was lying.

"Dad," I said, "can I go in for a second with Gabe?"

"Don't be long."

"I won't."

Gabriel's tiny apartment was messy and smelly.

"Maybe you ought to think about running with a different crowd," I said. "It doesn't sound like your future is worth much with the Red Scorpions."

He tossed his jacket over a chair and fingered the patch on the back. I saw tears in his eyes as he suddenly tore the patch off and threw it across the room. "I don't care if I ever wear this jacket again as long as I live, I'll tell you that," he said.

"That's probably not a bad idea," I said, but I shouldn't have said anything. I didn't really understand him or his life any more than he understood mine. The best I could hope for was that I could make him curious enough to ask me more.

My dad honked, and I moved toward the door. "You know what I'm going to do?" I asked. "I'm going to pray that you won't sleep well or have any peace until you find out more about God."

"About God? I don't wanna know anything about God. God hasn't helped me so far; why should He care now?"

"Maybe *you* need *Him* now. You always needed Him, only you didn't know it. He wants you. He wants to be your friend. There's a lot He wants to do for you."

"I don't want to hear any more, OK, Dallas? And don't waste your breath prayin' for me either."

"I can't promise that."

"Just don't do it."

I smiled at him. "What are we gonna do, fight about it? Watch me. I'll sucker punch you again to keep you from keeping me from praying for you."

He pursed his lips and shook his head. He opened the door. "Thanks for saving my hide anyway," he said. "And if you hear I'm not in school, don't tell anybody—not even Mike Ancona—where I am. OK?"

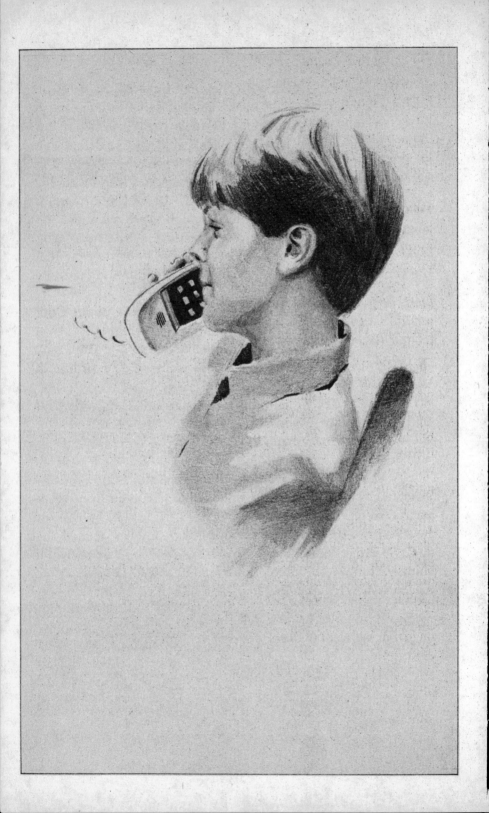

11

The Phone Call

For the next three days, the talk around my school was of the beating I had given Gabriel Irving and threat of the Red Scorpions against him. No one knew where he was, but I figured he had called in sick or had his mother call for him, because it was clear he wouldn't have been hard to find if school authorities were worried about him.

Finally, on the fourth day, I went to his apartment after school. I knew he was there because I could smell food cooking, and I knew his mother was at work. I kept knocking until he let me in. He looked mad.

"Before you say anything, O'Neil, I've got a couple of things to tell you, all right?"

I nodded.

"First, you can't stay long. My mother is comin' home in an hour and this spaghetti and the garlic bread has to be ready by then."

"Smells good. I can't believe you know how to do that."

"Yeah, well, I wouldn't know what to do with a salt block or a load of clothes either, so we're even. Anyway, I have something else to tell you. Quit prayin' for me."

"Can't do that. In fact, several of my friends are praying for you, and some people at church who don't even know you."

"See? I knew it! Now, I don't like that! Get off my case, will you? I haven't had a good night's sleep for days."

I sat down and smiled at him. "There's an easy way to make us back off, Gabe."

"How?"

"All we want you to do is find out more about God. We're not magicians, you know. If you're having trouble sleeping, it isn't so much because we're praying as that God is after you."

"What does He want?"

"He wants to forgive you."

"For what? What did I ever do to Him?"

"You ignored Him. He made you. You're His, but you run from Him."

Gabriel checked the stove and sat down. "You know," he said, "my aunt—my dad's sister—told me stuff like this before. She even got me to go to some Bible thing during the summer at her church in New York. It was kinda fun, but I was just a little kid then. They talked all the time about Jesus dyin' for our sins, but I didn't really know what they were talkin' about.

"I mean, I know I'm a bad guy and all that, but I never meant to be. It wasn't like I decided to be mean or sin or whatever you want to call it. I didn't make myself this way. Why do I need forgiveness from anybody?"

I started to answer, but he cut me off. "I wasn't really askin' you a question, Dallas. You know what I mean? I was just sort of saying why I'm not interested and why you should quit bugging me."

"Fair enough," I said, standing. "But you know what that means?"

"What?"

"We keep on praying for you."

"C'mon, man!"

"See ya, Gabe."

"Dallas! Just lay off me, OK? I know the routine. You can back off. It's my decision."

I was at the door. "That's the truest thing you've said so far."

"Then lay off."

I had written a list of verses he could read about how everyone is a sinner; that Jesus is the only way to God, and that forgiveness and life are available to anyone. "Do you have a Bible around here anywhere?"

"My mom has one somewhere!"

"Well, just look these up sometime. You know how to reach me."

"You can forget me reading the Bible too, Dallas. That's not gonna be my thing, OK?"

"Suit yourself."

"I will."

I smiled all the way home. I knew we were making progress. He was trying to sound angry and mean, but he was calling me by my first name, which told me something. And he didn't touch the list I left him, but at least he didn't throw it away, not while I was there anyway.

He was softening. I didn't know what would come of it, but I knew something was up.

The guys in the club who were praying for him were eager to get a report. I gave it to them the night before we played the Condors in our basketball league.

The guys thought I was either kidding, being chicken, or trying to get revenge when I said that the next time we played them I was going to put six-foot-four, two-hundred-pound Jack Bastable on little Mike Ancona, but I was serious.

It resulted in a very strange game. Our team was by far the favorite of the league, not expected to lose to anybody. But when the other teams and coaches and spectators saw Big Jack loping around in the back court trying to keep up with and frustrate little Mike—which he succeeded in doing—they laughed and wondered what we were up to.

Jack would bat away Mike's passes, and then usually Bugsy or Cory would streak to the other end and take a long pass for an easy lay-up. Before long I felt sorry for Mike, put Jack back on the low post, and moved out front to defend against Mike myself.

"Sorry to do that to you," I said, "but you never really paid for what you did to Ryan."

Mike didn't say anything for a long time, but after I stole the ball from him a couple of times and blocked one of his shots, he grew angrier and angrier. During a time-out he called me over. There was an edge to his voice. "You know, Gabe Irving's name is worth nothing with the Scorpions anymore. I hope you're happy."

"To help get him out of that crazy gang? Yeah, I am."

"Well, I'm their hottest new recruit."

"Mike, no! Don't do it!"

"They already gave me the money for my jacket."

"What do you have to do to join?"

"I already did it—to Ryan."

"Big stuff. Hassling someone smaller than you."

"You do what you've got to do."

"You know how Ryan feels now that you've had Jack Bastable in your face."

"Once I'm a full-fledged Red Scorpion, I won't have to be afraid of Jack Bastable or you or anyone else. I won't even be afraid of Gabriel Irving."

"Oh, so you admit you were scared of him. You pretended to be his friend and to be on his side to get him involved, because you didn't want to worry about him fighting you."

"Maybe. But I won't have to worry about him or anybody else soon."

"No. You won't have to worry about anyone except your buddies in the Red Scorpions."

Mike shook his head and walked away. He played a pretty good game after that until about the middle of the third quarter when he appeared distracted. He kept looking up into the stands, sometimes even when he was supposed to be getting open for a pass or a shot.

I stole a glance and saw Gabriel Irving in the last row of the main floor bleachers. I waved, and he nodded slightly, obviously not wanting to draw attention to himself.

By that time we had the game well in hand, and so I brought in all the subs. Ryan played Mike and dominated him the way he had on the playground. Mike threatened him a few times, but Ryan was beautiful. He didn't respond at all. He didn't look at him, say anything, make any gestures, nothing. That bothered Mike all the more.

Near the end of the game, which we won by twenty, I looked for Gabriel again. I couldn't find him anywhere.

After the game we celebrated with some Cokes, and then the ones who had been praying for Gabe stopped at my house. Before we broke up, Jimmy said, "Let's not quit now. Don't give up. If he's doing something brave like coming out in public, something's really going on with him."

As they left, we all agreed to keep praying.

I still had homework to finish, so I sat at the dining room table with my books and papers, trying to come down after an exciting, if easy, win. It was hard to concentrate on science and math, so I forced myself to stay awake and get it done.

When the last problem was solved I stacked everything in my backpack, hung it on the back door handle, and trudged up to my room. I was almost ready for bed when the phone rang. It was way past my bedtime already, and my parents had been asleep for an hour.

I raced into the hall and bounded down the stairs to the kitchen phone. "Hello?"

"Dallas, that you?"

"Yeah."

"Gabe."

"Hi."

"Am I callin' too late?"

"No." I was still panting.

"It's just that I've got a lot of questions for you, and if you wouldn't mind, I'd kinda like to get 'em answered right now. I'm gettin' real tired of bein' tired, and I'd like some sleep. If I get the answers I need, you can call off all your praying friends. Understand?"

"I think so."

"I'm giving in, Dallas. Giving up. Now do you understand?"

"Yeah, but really, Gabe, I don't want you to do this just to get me off your back. I don't really want to bug you into it."

"Listen, Dallas, maybe you bugged me to start thinkin' about it, and maybe you irritated me enough to get me to read some verses, but like I told you before, it's my decision. Nobody forces me into anything. Understand?"

I understood. And I hoped and prayed that before Gabriel Irving went to bed that night, he would understand too.

Moody Press, a ministry of the Moody Bible Institute, is designed for education, evangelization, and edification. If we may assist you in knowing more about Christ and the Christian life, please write us without obligation: Moody Press, c/o MLM, Chicago, Illinois 60610.